ACROSS THE

Nightingale Floor

THE SWORD OF THE WARRIOR

EPISODE
1

FIREBIRD
WHERE FANTASY TAKES FLIGHT™

OTORI
CLAN

MARUYAMA
CLAN

SEISHUU
CLAN

SHIRAKAWA
CLAN

TOHAN
CLAN

TALES
OF THE

OTORI

EPISODE
1

ACROSS THE
Nightingale Floor
THE SWORD OF THE WARRIOR

LIAN HEARN

FIREBIRD

AN IMPRINT OF PENGUIN GROUP (USA) INC.

HAYNER PUBLIC LIBRARY DISTRICT
ALTON, ILLINOIS

FIREBIRD
Published by the Penguin Group
Penguin Group (USA) Inc., 345 Hudson Street, New York, New York 10014, U.S.A.
Penguin Group (Canada), 10 Alcorn Avenue, Toronto, Ontario, Canada M4V 3B2
(a division of Pearson Penguin Canada Inc.)

Registered Offices: Penguin Books Ltd, 80 Strand, London WC2R 0RL, England

This is a work of fiction. Names, characters, places, and incidents either are the product of the
author's imagination or are used fictitiously, and any resemblance to actual persons, living or dead,
business establishments, events or locales is entirely coincidental.

The author gratefully acknowledges permission to quote from *From the Country of Eight Islands* by
Hiroaki Sato, translated by Burton Watson. Used by permission of Columbia University Press.

First published in the United States of America by Riverhead Books, published by The Berkley
Publishing Group, a division of Penguin Group (USA) Inc., 2002
Published by Firebird, an imprint of Penguin Group (USA) Inc., 2005

1 3 5 7 9 10 8 6 4 2

Copyright © Lian Hearn, 2002
Ornaments drawn by Jackie Aher
Clan symbols by Jackie Aher
Calligraphy drawn by Ms. Sugiyama Kazuko
Map by Xiangyi Mo

All rights reserved

THE LIBRARY OF CONGRESS HAS CATALOGUED THE RIVERHEAD EDITION AS FOLLOWS:
Hearn, Lian.
Across the nightingale floor / Lian Hearn.
p. cm.—(Tales of the Otori ; bk. I)
ISBN 1-57322-225-9
1. Teenage boys—Fiction. 2. Orphans—Fiction. 3. Japan—Fiction. I. Title.
PR9619.3.H3725 A65 2002   2002022339
823'.914—dc21

ISBN 0-14-240324-5

Printed in China

To E.

AUTHOR'S NOTE

The books that make up the *Tales of the Otori* are set in an imaginary country in a feudal period. Neither the setting nor the period is intended to correspond to any true historical era, though echoes of many Japanese customs and traditions will be found, and the landscape and seasons are those of Japan. Nightingale floors (*uguisubari*) are real inventions and were constructed around many residences and temples; the most famous examples can be seen in Kyoto at Nijo Castle and Chion'In. I have used Japanese names for places, but these have little connection with real places, apart from Hagi and Matsue, which are more or less in their true geographical positions. As for characters, they are all invented, apart from the artist Sesshu, who seemed impossible to replicate.

I hope I will be forgiven by purists for the liberties I have taken. My only excuse is that this is a work of the imagination.

THE THREE COUNTRIES

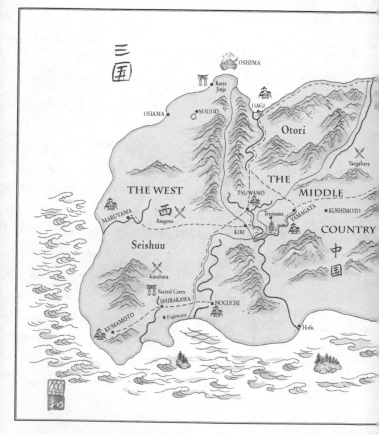

N 北

MATSUE

THE EAST

東 Tohan

•Hinode

•Mino

_____ fief boundaries

. . . . fief boundaries
           before Yaegahara

_ _ _ _ _ high road

battlefields

castletown

shrine

temple

CHARACTERS

The Clans

THE OTORI
(Middle Country; castle town: Hagi)

Otori Shigeru: rightful heir to the clan

Otori Takeshi: his younger brother, murdered by the Tohan clan **(d.)**

Otori Takeo: (born Tomasu) his adopted son

Otori Shigemori: Shigeru's father, killed at the battle of Yaegahara **(d.)**

Otori Ichiro: a distant relative, Shigeru and Takeo's teacher

Chiyo
Haruka: maids in the household

Shiro: a carpenter

Otori Shoichi: Shigeru's uncle, now lord of the clan
Otori Masahiro: Shoichi's younger brother
Otori Yoshitomi: Masahiro's son

Miyoshi Kahei: brothers, friends of Takeo
Miyoshi Gemba

Miyoshi Satoru: their father, captain of the guard in Hagi castle

Endo Chikara: a senior retainer

Terada Fumifusa: a pirate
Terada Fumio: his son, friend of Takeo

Ryoma: a fisherman, Masahiro's illegitimate son

THE TOHAN
(The East; castle town: Inuyama)

Iida Sadamu: lord of the clan
Iida Nariaki: Sadamu's cousin

Ando, Abe: Iida's retainers

Lord Noguchi: an ally
Lady Noguchi: his wife
Junko: a servant in Noguchi castle

THE SEISHUU
*(An alliance of several ancient families in the West;
main castle towns Kumamoto and Maruyama)*

Arai Daiichi: a warlord

Niwa Satoru: a retainer
Akita Tsutomu: a retainer
Sonoda Mitsuru: Akita's nephew
Maruyama Naomi: head of the Maruyama domain,
   Shigeru's lover

Mariko: her daughter
Sachie: her maid

Sugita Haruki: a retainer
Sugita Hiroshi: his nephew
Sakai Masaki: Hiroshi's cousin

Lord Shirakawa
Kaede: Shirakawa's eldest daughter, Lady Maruyama's cousin
Ai, Hana: Shirakawa's daughters

Ayame
Manami
Akane: maids in the household

Amano Tenzo: a Shirakawa retainer

Shoji Kiyoshi: senior retainer to Lord Shirakawa

The Tribe

THE MUTO FAMILY

Muto Kenji: Takeo's teacher, the Master
Muto Shizuka: Kenji's niece, Arai's mistress, and Kaede's
   companion
Zenko, Taku: her sons
Muto Seiko: Kenji's wife
Muto Yuki: their daughter
Muto Yuzuru: a cousin

Kana
Miyabi: maids

THE KIKUTA FAMILY

Kikuta Isamu: Takeo's real father (**d.**)
Kikuta Kotaro: his cousin, the Master
Kikuta Gosaburo: Kotaro's younger brother
Kikuta Akio: their nephew
Kikuta Hajime: a wrestler
Sadako: a maid

THE KURODA FAMILY

Kuroda Shintaro: a famous assassin
Kondo Kiichi
Imai Kazuo
Kudo Keiko

Others

Lord Fujiware: a nobleman, exiled from the capital
Mamoru: his protégé and companion
Ono Rieko: his cousin
Murita: a retainer

Matsuda Shingen: the abbot at Terayama
Kubo Makoto: a monk, Takeo's closest friend

Jin-emon: a bandit

Jiro: a farmer's son

Jo-An: an outcast

Horses

Raku: gray with black mane and tail, Takeo's first horse, given
by him to Kaede
Kyu: black, Shigeru's horse, disappeared in Inuyama
Aoi: black, half brother to Kyu
Ki: Amano's chestnut
Shun: Takeo's bay, a very clever horse

bold = main characters
(d.) = character died before the start of *Across the Nightingale Floor,*
Episode 1

天平五年癸酉、遣唐使の船、難波
を發ちて海に入る時に、親母の、子に
贈る歌一首　短歌を并せたり

秋萩を　妻問ふ鹿こそ　独子に
子持てりといへ　鹿児じもの　我が
独子の　草枕　旅にし行けば
竹珠を　しじに貫き垂り　齋瓮に
木綿取り垂でて　齋ひつつ
思ふ吾子　真幸くありこそ

「万葉集」巻九
一七九〇
一七九一

The deer that weds

The autumn bush clover

They say

Sires a single fawn

And this fawn of mine

This lone boy

Sets off on a journey

Grass for his pillow

ACROSS THE

Nightingale Floor

THE SWORD OF THE WARRIOR

·1·

My mother used to threaten to tear me into eight pieces if I knocked over the water bucket, or pretended not to hear her calling me to come home as the dusk thickened and the cicadas' shrilling increased. I would hear her voice, rough and fierce, echoing through the lonely valley. "Where's that wretched boy? I'll tear him apart when he gets back."

But when I did get back, muddy from sliding down the hillside, bruised from fighting, once bleeding great spouts of blood from a stone wound to the head (I still have the scar, like a silvered thumbnail), there would be the fire, and the smell of soup, and my mother's arms not tearing me apart but trying to hold me, clean my face, or straighten my hair, while

I twisted like a lizard to get away from her. She was strong from endless hard work, and not old: She'd given birth to me before she was seventeen, and when she held me I could see we had the same skin, although in other ways we were not much alike, she having broad, placid features, while mine, I'd been told (for we had no mirrors in the remote mountain village of Mino), were finer, like a hawk's. The wrestling usually ended with her winning, her prize being the hug I could not escape from. And her voice would whisper in my ears the words of blessing of the Hidden, while my stepfather grumbled mildly that she spoiled me, and the little girls, my half-sisters, jumped around us for their share of the hug and the blessing.

So I thought it was a manner of speaking. Mino was a peaceful place, too isolated to be touched by the savage battles of the clans. I had never imagined men and women could actually be torn into eight pieces, their strong, honey-colored limbs wrenched from their sockets and thrown down to the waiting dogs. Raised among the Hidden, with all their gentleness, I did not know men did such things to each other.

I turned fifteen and my mother began to lose our wrestling matches. I grew six inches in a year, and by the time I was sixteen I was taller than my stepfather. He grumbled more often, that I should settle down, stop roaming the mountain like a wild monkey, marry into one of the village families. I did not mind the idea of marriage to one of the girls I'd grown up with, and that summer I worked harder alongside him, ready to take my place among the men of the village. But every now and then I could not resist the lure of the mountain, and at the end of the day I slipped away, through the bamboo grove with its tall, smooth trunks and green slanting light, up the rocky path past the shrine of the mountain god, where the villagers left offerings of millet and oranges, into the forest of birch and cedar, where the cuckoo and the nightingale called enticingly, where I watched foxes and deer and heard the melancholy cry of kites overhead.

That evening I'd been right over the mountain to a place where the best mushrooms grew. I had a cloth full of them, the little white ones like threads, and the dark orange ones like fans. I was thinking how pleased my mother would be, and how the mushrooms would still my stepfather's scolding. I could already taste them on my tongue. As I ran through the bamboo and out into the rice fields where the red autumn lilies were already in flower, I thought I could smell cooking on the wind.

The village dogs were barking, as they often did at the end of the day. The smell grew stronger and turned acrid. I was not frightened, not then, but some premonition made my heart start to beat more quickly. There was a fire ahead of me.

Fires often broke out in the village: Almost everything we owned was made of wood or straw. But I could hear no shouting, no sounds of the buckets being passed from hand to hand, none of the usual cries and curses. The cicadas shrilled as loudly as ever; frogs were calling from the paddies. In the distance thunder echoed round the mountains. The air was heavy and humid.

I was sweating, but the sweat was turning cold on my forehead. I jumped across the ditch of the last terraced field and looked down to where my home had always been. The house was gone.

I went closer. Flames still crept and licked at the blackened beams. There was no sign of my mother or my sisters. I tried to call out, but my tongue had suddenly become too big for my mouth, and the smoke was choking me and making my eyes stream. The whole village was on fire, but where was everyone?

Then the screaming began.

It came from the direction of the shrine, around which most of the houses clustered. It was like the sound of a dog howling in pain, except the dog could speak human words, scream them in agony. I thought I recognized the prayers of the Hidden, and all the hair stood up on my neck and arms. Slipping like a ghost between the burning houses, I went towards the sound.

The village was deserted. I could not imagine where everyone had gone. I told myself they had run away: My mother had taken my sisters to the safety of the forest. I would go and find them just as soon as I had found out who was screaming. But as I stepped out of the alley into the main street I saw two men lying on the ground. A soft evening rain was beginning to fall and they looked surprised, as though they had no idea why they were lying there in the rain. They would never get up again, and it did not matter that their clothes were getting wet.

One of them was my stepfather.

At that moment the world changed for me. A kind of fog rose before my eyes, and when it cleared nothing seemed real. I felt I had crossed over to the other world, the one that lies alongside our own, that we visit in dreams. My stepfather was wearing his best clothes. The indigo cloth was dark with rain and blood. I was sorry they were spoiled: He had been so proud of them.

I stepped past the bodies, through the gates, and into the shrine. The rain was cool on my face. The screaming stopped abruptly.

Inside the grounds were men I did not know. They looked as if they were carrying out some ritual for a festival. They had cloths tied round their heads; they had taken off their jackets and their arms gleamed with sweat and rain. They were panting and grunting, grinning with white teeth, as though killing were as hard work as bringing in the rice harvest.

Water trickled from the cistern where you washed your hands and mouth to purify yourself on entering the shrine. Earlier, when the world was normal, someone must have lit incense in the great cauldron. The last of it drifted across the courtyard, masking the bitter smell of blood and death.

The man who had been torn apart lay on the wet stones. I could just make out the features on the severed head. It was Isao, the leader of the Hidden. His mouth was still open, frozen in a last contortion of pain.

The murderers had left their jackets in a neat pile against

a pillar. I could see clearly the crest of the triple oak leaf. These were Tohan men, from the clan capital of Inuyama. I remembered a traveler who had passed through the village at the end of the seventh month. He'd stayed the night at our house, and when my mother had prayed before the meal, he had tried to silence her. "Don't you know that the Tohan hate the Hidden and plan to move against us? Lord Iida has vowed to wipe us out," he whispered. My parents had gone to Isao the next day to tell him, but no one had believed them. We were far from the capital, and the power struggles of the clans had never concerned us. In our village the Hidden lived alongside everyone else, looking the same, acting the same, except for our prayers. Why would anyone want to harm us? It seemed unthinkable.

And so it still seemed to me as I stood frozen by the cistern. The water trickled and trickled, and I wanted to take some and wipe the blood from Isao's face and gently close his mouth, but I could not move. I knew at any moment the men from the Tohan clan would turn, and their gaze would fall on me, and they would tear me apart. They would have neither pity nor mercy. They were already polluted by death, having killed a man within the shrine itself.

In the distance I could hear with acute clarity the drumming sound of a galloping horse. As the hoofbeats drew nearer I had the sense of forward memory that comes to you in dreams. I knew who I was going to see, framed between the shrine gates. I had never seen him before in my life, but my mother had held him up to us as a sort of ogre with which to frighten us into obedience: Don't stray on the mountain, don't play by the river, or Iida will get you! I recognized him at once. Iida Sadamu, lord of the Tohan.

The horse reared and whinnied at the smell of blood. Iida sat as still as if he were cast in iron. He was clad from head to foot in black armor, his helmet crowned with antlers. He wore a short black beard beneath his cruel mouth. His eyes were bright, like a man hunting deer.

Those bright eyes met mine. I knew at once two things about him: first, that he was afraid of nothing in heaven or on earth; second, that he loved to kill for the sake of killing. Now that he had seen me, there was no hope.

His sword was in his hand. The only thing that saved me was the horse's reluctance to pass beneath the gate. It reared again, prancing backwards. Iida shouted. The men already inside the shrine turned and saw me, crying out in their rough Tohan accents. I grabbed the last of the incense, hardly noticing as it seared my hand, and ran out through the gates. As the horse shied towards me I thrust the incense against its flank. It reared over me, its huge feet flailing past my cheeks. I heard the hiss of the sword descending through the air. I was aware of the Tohan all around me. It did not seem possible that they could miss me, but I felt as if I had split in two. I saw Iida's sword fall on me, yet I was untouched by it. I lunged at the horse again. It gave a snort of pain and a savage series of bucks. Iida, unbalanced by the sword thrust that had somehow missed its target, fell forward over its neck and slid heavily to the ground.

Horror gripped me, and in its wake panic. I had unhorsed the lord of the Tohan. There would be no limit to the torture and pain to atone for such an act. I should have thrown myself to the ground and demanded death. But I knew I did not want to die. Something stirred in my blood, telling me I would not die before Iida. I would see him dead first.

I knew nothing of the wars of the clans, nothing of their rigid codes and their feuds. I had spent my whole life among the Hidden, who are forbidden to kill and taught to forgive each other. But at that moment Revenge took me as a pupil. I recognized her at once and learned her lessons instantly. She was what I desired; she would save me from the feeling that I was a living ghost. In that split second I took her into my heart. I kicked out at the man closest to me, getting him between the legs, sank my teeth into a hand that grabbed my wrist, broke away from them, and ran towards the forest.

Three of them came after me. They were bigger than I was and could run faster, but I knew the ground, and darkness was falling. So was the rain, heavier now, making the steep tracks of the mountain slippery and treacherous. Two of the men kept calling out to me, telling me what they would take great pleasure in doing to me, swearing at me in words whose meaning I could only guess, but the third ran silently, and he was the one I was afraid of. The other two might turn back after a while, get back to their maize liquor or whatever foul brew the Tohan got drunk on, and claim to have lost me on the mountain, but this other one would never give up. He would pursue me forever until he had killed me.

As the track steepened near the waterfall, the two noisy ones dropped back a bit, but the third quickened his pace as an animal will when it runs uphill. We passed by the shrine;

a bird was pecking at the millet and it flew off with a flash of green and white in its wings. The track curved a little round the trunk of a huge cedar, and as I ran with stone legs and sobbing breath past the tree, someone rose out of its shadow and blocked the path in front of me.

I ran straight into him. He grunted as though I had winded him, but he held me immediately. He looked in my face and I saw something flicker in his eyes: surprise, recognition. Whatever it was, it made him grip me more tightly. There was no getting away this time. I heard the Tohan man stop, then the heavy footfalls of the other two coming up behind him.

"Excuse me, sir," said the man I feared, his voice steady. "You have apprehended the criminal we were chasing. Thank you."

The man holding me turned me round to face my pursuers. I wanted to cry out to him, to plead with him, but I knew it was no use. I could feel the soft fabric of his clothes, the smoothness of his hands. He was some sort of lord, no doubt, just like Iida. They were all of the same cut. He would do nothing to help me. I kept silent, thought of the prayers my mother had taught me, thought fleetingly of the bird.

"What has this criminal done?" the lord asked.

The man in front of me had a long face, like a wolf's. "Excuse me," he said again, less politely. "That is no concern of yours. It is purely the business of Iida Sadamu and the Tohan."

"Unnh!" the lord grunted. "Is that so? And who might you be to tell me what is and what is not my concern?"

"Just hand him over!" the wolf man snarled, all politeness gone. As he stepped forward, I knew suddenly that the lord was not going to hand me over. With one neat movement he twisted me behind his back and let go of me. I heard for the second time in my life the hiss of the warrior's sword as it is brought to life. The wolf man drew out a knife. The other two had poles. The lord raised the sword with both hands, sidestepped under one of the poles, lopped off the head of the man holding it, came back at the wolf man, and took off the right arm, still holding the knife.

It happened in a moment, yet took an eternity. It happened in the last of the light, in the rain, but when I close my eyes I can still see every detail.

The headless body fell with a thud and a gush of blood, the head rolling down the slope. The third man dropped his stick and ran backwards, calling for help. The wolf man was on his knees, trying to stanch the blood from the stump at his elbow. He did not groan or speak.

The lord wiped the sword and returned it to its sheath in his belt. "Come on," he said to me.

I stood shaking, unable to move. This man had appeared from nowhere. He had killed in front of my eyes to save my life. I dropped to the ground before him, trying to find the words to thank him.

"Get up," he said. "The rest of them will be after us in a moment."

"I can't leave," I managed to say. "I must find my mother."

"Not now. Now is the time for us to run!" He pulled me to my feet, and began to hurry me up the slope. "What happened down there?"

"They burned the village and killed . . ." The memory of my stepfather came back to me and I could not go on.

"Hidden?"

"Yes," I whispered.

"It's happening all over the fief. Iida is stirring up hatred against them everywhere. I suppose you're one of them?"

"Yes." I was shivering. Although it was still late summer and the rain was warm, I had never felt so cold. "But that wasn't only why they were after me. I caused Lord Iida to fall from his horse."

To my amazement the lord began to snort with laughter. "That would have been worth seeing! But it places you doubly in danger. It's an insult he'll have to wipe out. Still, you are under my protection now. I won't let Iida take you from me."

"You saved my life," I said. "It belongs to you from this day on."

For some reason that made him laugh again. "We have a long walk, on empty stomachs and with wet garments. We must be over the range before daybreak, when they will come after us." He strode off at great speed, and I ran after him, willing my legs not to shake, my teeth not to chatter. I didn't even know his name, but I wanted him to be proud of me, never to regret that he had saved my life.

"I am Otori Shigeru," he said as we began the climb to the pass. "Of the Otori clan, from Hagi. But while I'm on the road I don't use that name, so don't you use it either."

Hagi was as distant as the moon to me, and although I had heard of the Otori, I knew nothing about them except that they had been defeated by the Tohan at a great battle ten years earlier on the plain of Yaegahara.

"What's your name, boy?"

"Tomasu."

"That's a common name among the Hidden. Better get rid of it." He said nothing for a while, and then spoke briefly out of the darkness. "You can be called Takeo."

And so between the waterfall and the top of the mountain I lost my name, became someone new, and joined my destiny with the Otori.

❖

Dawn found us, cold and hungry, in the village of Hinode, famous for its hot springs. I was already farther from my own house than I had ever been in my life. All I knew of Hinode was what the boys in my village said: that the men were cheats and the women were as hot as the springs and would lie down with you for the price of a cup of wine. I didn't have the chance to find out if either was true. No one dared to cheat Lord Otori, and the only woman I saw was the innkeeper's wife who served our meals.

I was ashamed of how I looked, in the old clothes my

mother had patched so often it was impossible to tell what color they'd been to start with, filthy, bloodstained. I couldn't believe that the lord expected me to sleep in the inn with him. I thought I would stay in the stables. But he seemed not to want to let me too often out of his sight. He told the woman to wash my clothes and sent me to the hot spring to scrub myself. When I came back, almost asleep from the effect of the hot water after the sleepless night, the morning meal was laid out in the room, and he was already eating. He gestured to me to join him. I knelt on the floor and said the prayers we always used before the first meal of the day.

"You can't do that," Lord Otori said through a mouthful of rice and pickles. "Not even alone. If you want to live, you have to forget that part of your life. It is over forever." He swallowed and took another mouthful. "There are better things to die for."

I suppose a true believer would have insisted on the prayers anyway. I wondered if that was what the dead men of my village would have done. I remembered the way their eyes had looked blank and surprised at the same time. I stopped praying. My appetite left me.

"Eat," the lord said, not unkindly. "I don't want to carry you all the way to Hagi."

I forced myself to eat a little so he would not despise me. Then he sent me to tell the woman to spread out the beds. I felt uncomfortable giving orders to her, not only because I thought she would laugh at me and ask me if I'd lost the use of my hands, but also because something was happening to my voice. I could feel it draining away from me, as though words were too weak to frame what my eyes had seen. Anyway, once she'd grasped what I meant, she bowed almost as low as she had to Lord Otori and bustled along to obey.

Lord Otori lay down and closed his eyes. He seemed to fall asleep immediately.

I thought I, too, would sleep at once, but my mind kept jumping around, shocked and exhausted. My burned hand was throbbing and I could hear everything around me with an unusual and slightly alarming clarity—every word that was spoken in the kitchens, every sound from the town. Over and over my thoughts kept returning to my mother and the little girls. I told myself I had not actually seen them dead. They had probably run away; they would be safe. Everyone liked my mother in our village. She would not have chosen death. Although she had been born into the Hidden, she was not a fanatic. She lit incense in the shrine and took offerings to the god of the mountain. Surely my mother, with her broad face, her rough hands, and her honey-colored skin, was not dead, was not lying somewhere under the sky, her sharp eyes empty and surprised, her daughters next to her!

My own eyes were not empty: They were shamefully full of tears. I buried my face in the mattress and tried to will the tears away. I could not keep my shoulders from shaking or my breath from coming in rough sobs. After a few moments I felt a hand on my shoulder and Lord Otori said quietly, "Death comes suddenly and life is fragile and brief. No one can alter this, either by prayers or spells. Children cry about it, but men and women do not cry. They have to endure."

His own voice broke on this last word. Lord Otori was as grief-stricken as I was. His face was clenched but the tears still trickled from his eyes. I knew who I wept for, but I did not dare question him.

I must have fallen asleep, for I was dreaming I was at home, eating supper out of a bowl as familiar to me as my own hands. There was a black crab in the soup, and it jumped out of the bowl and ran away into the forest. I ran after it, and after a while I didn't know where I was. I tried to cry out "I'm lost!" but the crab had taken away my voice.

I woke to find Lord Otori shaking me.

"Get up!"

I could hear that it had stopped raining. The light told me it was the middle of the day. The room seemed close and sticky, the air heavy and still. The straw matting smelled slightly sour.

"I don't want Iida coming after me with a hundred warriors just because a boy made him fall off his horse," Lord Otori grumbled good-naturedly. "We must move on quickly."

I didn't say anything. My clothes, washed and dried, lay on the floor. I put them on silently.

"Though how you dared stand up to Sadamu when you're too scared to say a word to me . . ."

I wasn't exactly scared of him—more like in complete awe. It was as if one of God's angels, or one of the spirits of the forest, or a hero from the old days, had suddenly appeared in front of me and taken me under his protection. I could hardly have told you then what he looked like, for I did not dare look at him directly. When I did sneak a glance at him, his face in repose was calm—not exactly stern, but expressionless. I did not then know the way it was transformed by his smile. He was perhaps thirty years old, or a little younger, well above medium height, broad-shouldered. His hands were light-skinned, almost white, well formed, and with long, restless fingers that seemed made to shape themselves around the sword's handle.

They did that now, lifting the sword from where it lay on the matting. The sight of it sent a shudder through me. I imagined it had known the intimate flesh, the lifeblood, of many men—had heard their last cries. It terrified and fascinated me.

"Jato," Lord Otori said, noticing my gaze. He laughed and patted the shabby black sheath. "In traveling clothes, like me. At home we both dress more elegantly!"

Jato, I repeated under my breath. The snake sword, which had saved my life by taking life.

We left the inn and resumed our journey past the sulfur-smelling hot springs of Hinode and up another mountain. The rice paddies gave way to bamboo groves, just like the ones around my village; then came chestnuts, maples, and cedars. The forest steamed from the warmth of the sun, although it was so dense that little sunlight penetrated to us below. Twice, snakes slithered out of our path, one the little black adder and another, larger one the color of tea. It seemed to roll like a hoop, and it leaped into the undergrowth as though it knew Jato might lop off its head. Cicadas sang stridently, and the min-min moaned with head-splitting monotony.

We went at a brisk pace despite the heat. Sometimes Lord Otori would outstride me and I would toil up the track as if utterly alone, hearing only his footsteps ahead, and then come upon him at the top of the pass, gazing out over the view of mountains, and beyond them more mountains stretching away, and everywhere the impenetrable forest.

He seemed to know his way through this wild country. We walked for long days and slept only a few hours at night, sometimes in a solitary farmhouse, sometimes in a deserted mountain hut. Apart from the places we stopped at, we met few people on this lonely road: a woodcutter, two girls collecting mushrooms who ran away at the sight of us, a monk on a journey to a distant temple. After a few days we crossed the spine of the country. We still had steep hills to climb, but we descended more frequently. The sea became visible, a distant glint at first, then a broad silky expanse with islands jutting up like drowned mountains. I had never seen it before, and I couldn't stop looking at it. Sometimes it seemed like a high wall about to topple across the land.

My hand healed slowly, leaving a silver scar across my right palm.

The villages became larger, until we finally stopped for the night in what could only be called a town. It was on the high road between Inuyama and the coast and had many inns and eating places. We were still in Tohan territory, and the triple oak leaf was everywhere, making me afraid to go out in the streets, yet I felt the people at the inn recognized Lord Otori in some way. The usual respect people paid to him was tinged by something deeper, some old loyalty that had to be kept hidden. They treated me with affection, even though I did not speak to them. I had not spoken for days, not even to Lord Otori. It did not seem to bother him much. He was a silent man himself, wrapped up in his own thoughts, but every now and then I would sneak a look at him and find him studying me with an expression on his face that might have been pity. He would seem to be about to speak, then he'd grunt and mutter, "Never mind, never mind, things can't be helped."

The servants were full of gossip, and I liked listening to them. They were deeply interested in a woman who had arrived the night before and was staying another night. She was traveling alone to Inuyama, apparently to meet Lord Iida himself, with servants, naturally, but no husband or brother or father. She was very beautiful though quite old, thirty at least, very nice, kind, and polite to everyone but—traveling alone! What a mystery! The cook claimed to know that she was recently widowed and was going to join her son in the capital, but the chief maid said that was nonsense, the woman had never had children, never been married, and then the horse boy, who was stuffing his face with his supper, said he had heard from the palanquin bearers that she had had two children, a boy who died and a girl who was a hostage in Inuyama.

The maids sighed and murmured that even wealth and high birth could not protect you from fate, and the horse boy said, "At least the girl lives, for they are Maruyama, and they inherit through the female line."

This news brought a stir of surprise and understanding

and renewed curiosity about Lady Maruyama, who held her land in her own right, the only domain to be handed down to daughters, not to sons.

"No wonder she dares to travel alone," the cook said.

Carried away by his success, the horse boy went on, "But Lord Iida finds this offensive. He seeks to take over her territory, either by force or, they say, by marriage."

The cook gave him a clip round the ear. "Watch your words! You never know who's listening!"

"We were Otori once, and will be again," the boy muttered.

The chief maid saw me hanging about in the doorway and beckoned to me to come in. "Where are you traveling to? You must have come a long way!"

I smiled and shook my head. One of the maids, passing on her way to the guest rooms, patted me on the arm and said, "He doesn't talk. Shame, isn't it?"

"What happened?" the cook said. "Someone throw dust in your mouth like the Ainu dog?"

They were teasing me, not unkindly, when the maid came back, followed by a man I gathered was one of the Maruyama servants, wearing on his jacket the crest of the mountain enclosed in a circle. To my surprise he addressed me in polite language. "My lady wishes to talk to you."

I wasn't sure if I should go with him, but he had the face of an honest man, and I was curious to see the mysterious woman for myself. I followed him along the passageway and through the courtyard. He stepped onto the veranda and knelt at the door to the room. He spoke briefly, then turned to me and beckoned to me to step up.

I snatched a rapid glance at her and then fell to my knees and bowed my head to the floor. I was sure I was in the presence of a princess. Her hair reached the ground in one long sweep of black silkiness. Her skin was as pale as snow. She wore robes of deepening shades of cream, ivory, and dove gray embroidered with red and pink peonies. She had a stillness about her that made me think first of the deep pools of the mountain and then, suddenly, of the tempered steel of Jato, the snake sword.

"They tell me you don't talk," she said, her voice as quiet and clear as water.

I felt the compassion of her gaze, and the blood rushed to my face.

"You can talk to me," she went on. Reaching forward,

she took my hand and with her finger drew the sign of the Hidden on my palm. It sent a shock through me, like the sting of a nettle. I could not help pulling my hand away.

"Tell me what you saw," she said, her voice no less gentle but insistent. When I didn't reply she whispered, "It was Iida Sadamu, wasn't it?"

I looked at her almost involuntarily. She was smiling, but without mirth.

"And you are from the Hidden," she added.

Lord Otori had warned me against giving myself away. I thought I had buried my old self, along with my name, Tomasu. But in front of this woman I was helpless. I was about to nod my head, when I heard Lord Otori's footsteps cross the courtyard. I realized that I recognized him by his tread, and I knew that a woman followed him, as well as the man who had spoken to me. And then I realized that if I paid attention, I could hear everything in the inn around me. I heard the horse boy get up and leave the kitchen. I heard the gossip of the maids, and knew each one from her voice. This acuteness of hearing, which had been growing slowly ever since I'd ceased to speak, now came over me with a flood of sound. It was almost unbearable, as if I had the worst of fevers. I wondered if the woman in front of me was a sorceress who had bewitched me. I did not dare lie to her, but I could not speak.

I was saved by the woman coming into the room. She knelt before Lady Maruyama and said quietly, "His lordship is looking for the boy."

"Ask him to come in," the lady replied. "And, Sachie, would you kindly bring the tea utensils?"

Lord Otori stepped into the room, and he and Lady Maruyama exchanged deep bows of respect. They spoke politely to each other like strangers, and she did not use his name, yet I had the feeling they knew each other well. There was a tension between them that I would understand later, but which then only made me more ill at ease.

"The maids told me about the boy who travels with you," she said. "I wished to see him for myself."

"Yes, I am taking him to Hagi. He is the only survivor of a massacre. I did not want to leave him to Sadamu." He did not seem inclined to say anything else, but after a while he added, "I have given him the name of Takeo."

She smiled at this—a real smile. "I'm glad," she said. "He has a certain look about him."

"Do you think so? I thought it too."

Sachie came back with a tray, a teakettle, and a bowl. I could see them clearly as she placed them on the matting, at the same level as my eyes. The bowl's glaze held the green of the forest, the blue of the sky.

"One day you will come to Maruyama to my grandmother's teahouse," the lady said. "There we can do the ceremony as it should be performed. But for now we will have to make do as best we can."

She poured the hot water, and a bittersweet smell wafted up from the bowl. "Sit up, Takeo," she said.

She was whisking the tea into a green foam. She passed the bowl to Lord Otori. He took it in both hands, turned it three times, drank from it, wiped the lip with his thumb, and handed it with a bow back to her. She filled it again and passed it to me. I carefully did everything the lord had done, lifted it to my lips, and drank the frothy liquid. Its taste was bitter, but it was clearing to the head. It steadied me a little. We never had anything like this in Mino: Our tea was made from twigs and mountain herbs.

I wiped the place I had drunk from and handed the bowl back to Lady Maruyama, bowing clumsily. I was afraid Lord

Otori would notice and be ashamed of me, but when I glanced at him his eyes were fixed on the lady.

She then drank herself. The three of us sat in silence. There was a feeling in the room of something sacred, as though we had just taken part in the ritual meal of the Hidden. A wave of longing swept over me for my home, my family, my old life, but although my eyes grew hot, I did not allow myself to weep. I would learn to endure.

On my palm I could still feel the trace of Lady Maruyama's fingers.

The inn was far larger and more luxurious than any of the other places we had stayed during our swift journey through the mountains, and the food we ate that night was unlike anything I had ever tasted. We had eel in a spicy sauce, and sweet fish from the local streams, many servings of rice, whiter than anything in Mino, where if we ate rice three times a year we were lucky. I drank rice wine for the first time. Lord Otori was in high spirits—"floating," as my mother used to say—his silence and grief dispelled, and the wine worked its cheerful magic on me too.

When we had finished eating he told me to go to bed: He was going to walk outside awhile to clear his head. The maids came and prepared the room. I lay down and listened to the sounds of the night. The eel, or the wine, had made me restless and I could hear too much. Every distant noise made me start awake. I could hear the dogs of the town bark from time to time, one starting, the others joining in. After a while I felt I could recognize each one's distinctive voice. I thought about dogs, how they sleep with their ears twitching and how only some noises disturb them. I would have to learn to be like them or I would never sleep again.

When I heard the temple bells toll at midnight, I got up and went to the privy. The sound of my own piss was like a waterfall. I poured water over my hands from the cistern in the courtyard and stood for a moment, listening.

It was a still, mild night, coming up to the full moon of the eighth month. The inn was silent: Everyone was in bed and asleep. Frogs were croaking from the river and the rice fields, and once or twice I heard an owl hoot. As I stepped quietly onto the veranda I heard Lord Otori's voice. For a moment I thought he must have returned to the room and was speaking to me, but a woman's voice answered him. It was Lady Maruyama.

I knew I should not listen. It was a whispered conversation that no one could hear but me. I went into the room, slid the door shut, and lay down on the mattress, willing myself to fall asleep. But my ears had a longing for sound that I could not deny, and every word dropped clearly into them.

They spoke of their love for each other, their few meetings, their plans for the future. Much of what they said was guarded and brief, and much of it I did not understand then. I learned that Lady Maruyama was on her way to the capital to see her daughter, and that she feared Iida would again insist on marriage. His own wife was unwell and not expected to live. The only son she had borne him, also sickly, was a disappointment to him.

"You will marry no one but me," he whispered, and she replied, "It is my only desire. You know it." He then swore to her he would never take a wife, nor lie with any woman, unless it were she, and he spoke of some strategy he had, but did not spell it out. I heard my own name and conceived that it involved me in some way. I realized there was a long-existing enmity between him and Iida that went all the way back to the battle of Yaegahara.

"We will die on the same day," he said. "I cannot live in a world that does not include you."

Then the whispering turned to other sounds, those of passion between a man and a woman. I put my fingers in my ears. I knew about desire, had satisfied my own with the other boys of my village, or with girls in the brothel, but I knew nothing of love. Whatever I heard, I vowed to myself I would never speak of it. I would keep these secrets as close as the Hidden keep theirs. I was thankful I had no voice.

I did not see the lady again. We left early the next morning, an hour or so after sunrise. It was already warm; monks were sprinkling water in the temple cloisters and the air smelled of dust. The maids at the inn had brought us tea, rice, and soup before we left, one of them stifling a yawn as she set the dishes before me, and then apologizing to me and laughing. It was the girl who had patted me on the arm the day before, and when we left she came out to cry, "Good luck, little lord! Good journey! Don't forget us here!"

I wished I was staying another night. The lord laughed at it, teasing me and saying he would have to protect me from the girls in Hagi. He could hardly have slept the previous night, yet his high spirits were still evident. He strode along the highway with more energy than usual. I thought we would take the post road to Yamagata, but instead we went through the town, following a river smaller than the wide one that flowed alongside the main road. We crossed it where it ran fast and narrow between boulders, and headed once more up the side of a mountain.

We had brought food with us from the inn for the day's walk, for once we were beyond the small villages along the river, we saw no one. It was a narrow, lonely path, and a steep climb. When we reached the top we stopped and ate. It was late afternoon, and the sun sent slanting shadows across the plain below us. Beyond it, towards the East, lay range after range of mountains turning indigo and steel-gray.

"That is where the capital is," Lord Otori said, following my gaze.

I thought he meant Inuyama, and I was puzzled.

He saw it and went on, "No, the real capital, of the whole country—where the Emperor lives. Way beyond the farthest mountain range. Inuyama lies to the southeast." He pointed back in the direction we had come. "It's because we are so far from the capital, and the Emperor is so weak, that warlords like Iida can do as they please." His mood was turning somber again. "And below us is the scene of the Otori's worst defeat, where my father was killed. That is Yaegahara. The Otori were betrayed by the Noguchi, who changed sides and joined Iida. More than ten thousand died." He looked at me and said, "I know what it is like to see those closest to you slaughtered. I was not much older than you are now."

I stared out at the empty plain. I could not imagine what a battle was like. I thought of the blood of ten thousand men soaking into the earth of Yaegahara. In the moist haze the sun was turning red, as if it had drawn up the blood from the land. Kites wheeled below us, calling mournfully.

"I did not want to go to Yamagata," Lord Otori said as we began to descend the path. "Partly because I am too well known there, and for other reasons. One day I will tell them to you. But it means we will have to sleep outside tonight, grass for our pillow, for there is no town near enough to stay in. We will cross the fief border by a secret route I know, and then we will be in Otori territory, safely out of reach of Sadamu."

I did not want to spend the night on the lonely plain. I was afraid of ten thousand ghosts, and of the ogres and goblins that dwelled in the forest around it. The murmur of a stream sounded to me like the voice of the water spirit, and every time a fox barked or an owl hooted I came awake, my pulse racing. At one stage the earth itself shook, in a slight tremor, making the trees rustle and dislodging stones somewhere in the distance. I thought I could hear the voices of the dead, calling for revenge, and I tried to pray, but all I could feel was a vast emptiness. The secret god, whom the Hidden worship, had been dispersed with my family. Away from them, I had no contact with him.

Next to me Lord Otori slept as peacefully as if he had been in the guest room of the inn. Yet, I knew that, even more than I was, he would have been aware of the demands of the dead. I thought with trepidation about the world I was entering—a world that I knew nothing about, the world of the clans, with their strict rules and harsh codes. I was entering it on the whim of this lord, whose sword had beheaded a man in front of my eyes, who as good as owned me. I shivered in the damp night air.

We rose before dawn and, as the sky was turning gray, crossed the river that marked the boundary to the Otori domain.

After Yaegahara the Otori, who had formerly ruled the whole of the Middle Country, were pushed back by the Tohan into a narrow strip of land between the last range of mountains and the northern sea. On the main post road the barrier was guarded by Iida's men, but in this wild isolated country there were many places where it was possible to slip across the border, and most of the peasants and farmers still considered themselves Otori and had no love for the Tohan. Lord Otori told me all this as we walked that day, the sea now always on our right-hand side. He also told me about the countryside, pointed out the farming methods used, the dikes built for irrigation, the nets the fishermen wove, the way they extracted salt from the sea. He was interested in everything and knew about everything. Gradually the path became a road and grew busier. Now there were farmers going to market at the next village, carrying yams and greens, eggs and dried mushrooms, lotus root and bamboo. We stopped at the market and bought new straw sandals, for ours were falling to pieces.

That night, when we came to the inn, everyone there knew Lord Otori. They ran out to greet him with exclamations of delight, and flattened themselves to the ground in front of him. The best rooms were prepared, and at the evening meal course after course of delicious food appeared. He seemed to change before my eyes. Of course I had known he was of high birth, of the warrior class, but I still had no idea exactly who he was or what part he played in the hierarchy of the clan. However, it was dawning on me that it must be exalted. I became even more shy in his presence. I felt that everyone was looking at me sideways, wondering what I was doing, longing to send me packing with a cuff on the ear.

The next morning he was wearing clothes befitting his station; horses were waiting for us, and four or five retainers. They grinned at each other a bit when they saw I knew nothing about horses, and they seemed surprised when Lord Otori told one of them to take me on the back of his horse, although of course none of them dared say anything. On the journey they tried to talk to me—they asked me where I'd come from and what my name was—but when they found I was mute, they decided I was stupid, and deaf too. They talked loudly to me in simple words, using sign language.

I didn't care much for jogging along on the back of the horse. The only horse I'd ever been close to was Iida's, and I thought all horses might bear me a grudge for the pain I'd caused that one. And I kept wondering what I would do when we got to Hagi. I imagined I would be some kind of servant, in the garden or the stables. But it turned out Lord Otori had other plans for me.

On the afternoon of the third day since the night we had spent on the edge of Yaegahara, we came to the city of Hagi, the castle town of the Otori. It was built on an island flanked by two rivers and the sea. From a spit of land to the town itself ran the longest stone bridge I had ever seen. It had four arches, through which the ebbing tide raced, and walls of perfectly fitted stone. I thought it must have been made by sorcery, and when the horses stepped onto it I couldn't help closing my eyes. The roar of the river was like thunder in my ears, but beneath it I could hear something else—a kind of low keening that made me shiver.

At the center of the bridge Lord Otori called to me. I slipped from the horse's back and went to where he had halted. A large boulder had been set into the parapet. It was engraved with characters.

"Can you read, Takeo?"

I shook my head.

"Bad luck for you. You will have to learn!" He laughed.

"And I think your teacher will make you suffer! You'll be sorry you left your wild life in the mountains."

He read aloud to me: "'The Otori clan welcomes the just and the loyal. Let the unjust and the disloyal beware.'" Beneath the characters was the crest of the heron.

I walked alongside his horse to the end of the bridge. "They buried the stonemason alive beneath the boulder," Lord Otori remarked offhandedly, "so he would never build another bridge to rival this one, and so he could guard his work forever. You can hear his ghost at night talking to the river."

Not only at night. It chilled me, thinking of the sad ghost imprisoned within the beautiful thing he had made, but then we were in the town itself, and the sounds of the living drowned out the dead.

Hagi was the first city I had ever been in, and it seemed vast and overwhelmingly confusing. My head rang with sounds: cries of street sellers, the clack of looms from within the narrow houses, the sharp blows of stonemasons, the snarling bite of saws, and many that I'd never heard before and could not identify. One street was full of potters, and the smell of the clay and the kiln hit my nostrils. I'd never heard a potter's wheel before, or the roar of the furnace. And lying beneath all the other sounds were the chatter, cries, curses, and laughter of human beings, just as beneath the smells lay the ever-present stench of their waste.

Above the houses loomed the castle, built with its back to the sea. For a moment I thought that was where we were heading, and my heart sank, so grim and foreboding did it look, but we turned to the east, following the Nishigawa river to where it joined the Higashigawa. To our left lay an area of winding streets and canals where tiled-roofed walls surrounded many large houses, just visible through the trees.

The sun had disappeared behind dark clouds, and the air smelled of rain. The horses quickened their step, knowing they were nearly home. At the end of the street a wide gate stood open. The guards had come out from the guardhouse next to it and dropped to their knees, heads bowed, as we went past.

Lord Otori's horse lowered its head and rubbed it roughly against me. It whinnied and another horse answered from the stables. I held the bridle, and the lord dismounted. The retainers took the horses and led them away.

He strode through the garden toward the house. I stood

for a moment, hesitant, not knowing whether to follow him or go with the men, but he turned and called my name, beckoning to me.

The garden was full of trees and bushes that grew, not like the wild trees of the mountain, dense and pressed together, but each in its own place, sedate and well trained. And yet, every now and then I thought I caught a glimpse of the mountain as if it had been captured and brought here in miniature.

It was full of sound too—the sound of water flowing over rocks, trickling from pipes. We stopped to wash our hands at the cistern, and the water ran away tinkling like a bell, as though it were enchanted.

The house servants were already waiting on the veranda to greet their master. I was surprised there were so few, but I learned later that Lord Otori lived in great simplicity. There were three young girls, an older woman, and a man of about fifty years. After the bows the girls withdrew and the two old people gazed at me in barely disguised amazement.

"He is so like . . . !" the woman whispered.

"Uncanny!" the man agreed, shaking his head.

Lord Otori was smiling as he stepped out of his sandals

and entered the house. "I met him in the dark! I had no idea till the following morning. It's just a passing likeness."

"No, far more than that," the old woman said, leading me inside. "He is the very image." The man followed, gazing at me with lips pressed together as though he had just bitten on a pickled plum—as though he foresaw nothing but trouble would spring from my introduction into the house.

"Anyway, I've called him Takeo," the lord said over his shoulder. "Heat the bath and find clothes for him."

The old man grunted in surprise.

"Takeo!" the woman exclaimed. "But what's your real name?"

When I said nothing, just shrugged and smiled, the man snapped, "He's a half-wit!"

"No, he can talk perfectly well," Lord Otori returned impatiently. "I've heard him talk. But he saw some terrible things that silenced him. When the shock has faded he'll speak again."

"Of course he will," said the old woman, smiling and nodding at me. "You come with Chiyo. I'll look after you."

"Forgive me, Lord Shigeru," the old man said stubbornly—I guessed these two had known the lord since he was a child, and had brought him up—"but what are your plans for the boy? Is he to be found work in the kitchen or the garden? Is he to be apprenticed? Has he any skills?"

"I intend to adopt him," Lord Otori replied. "You can start the procedures tomorrow, Ichiro."

There was a long moment of silence. Ichiro looked stunned, but he could not have been more flabbergasted than I was. Chiyo seemed to be trying not to smile. Then they both spoke together. She murmured an apology and let the old man speak first.

"It's very unexpected," he said huffily. "Did you plan this before you left on your journey?"

"No, it happened by chance. You know my grief after my brother's death and how I've sought relief in travel. I found this boy, and since then somehow every day the grief seems more bearable."

Chiyo clasped her hands together. "Fate sent him to you. As soon as I set eyes on you, I knew you were changed—healed in some way. Of course no one can ever replace Lord Takeshi. . . ."

Takeshi! So Lord Otori had given me a name like that of his dead brother. And he would adopt me into the family.

The Hidden speak of being reborn through water. I had been reborn through the sword.

"Lord Shigeru, you are making a terrible mistake," Ichiro said bluntly. "The boy is a nobody, a commoner. . . . What will the clan think? Your uncles will never allow it. Even to make the request is an insult."

"Look at him," Lord Otori said. "Whoever his parents were, someone in his past was not a commoner. Anyway, I rescued him from the Tohan. Iida wanted him killed. Since I saved his life, he belongs to me, and so I must adopt him. To be safe from the Tohan he must have the protection of the clan. I killed a man for him, possibly two."

"A high price. Let's hope it goes no higher," Ichiro snapped. "What had he done to attract Iida's attention?"

"He was in the wrong place at the wrong time, nothing more. There's no need to go into his history. He can be a distant relative of my mother's. Make something up."

"The Tohan have been persecuting the Hidden," Ichiro said astutely. "Tell me he's not one of them."

"If he was, he is no longer," Lord Otori replied with a sigh. "All that is in the past. It's no use arguing, Ichiro. I have given my word to protect this boy, and nothing will make me change my mind. Besides, I have grown fond of him."

"No good will come of it," Ichiro said.

The old man and the younger one stared at each other for a moment. Lord Otori made an impatient movement with his hand, and Ichiro lowered his eyes and bowed reluctantly. I thought how useful it would be to be a lord—to know that you would always get your own way in the end.

There was a sudden gust of wind, the shutters creaked, and with the sound the world became unreal for me again. It was as if a voice spoke inside my head: This is what you are to become. I wanted desperately to turn back time to the day before I went mushrooming on the mountain—back to my old life with my mother and my people. But I knew my childhood lay behind me, done with, out of reach forever. I had to become a man and endure whatever was sent me.

With these noble thoughts in my mind I followed Chiyo to the bathhouse. She obviously had no idea of the decision I'd come to: She treated me like a child, making me take off my clothes and scrubbing me all over before leaving me to soak in the scalding water. Later, she came back with a light cotton robe and told me to put it on. I did exactly as I was told. What else could I do? She rubbed my hair with a towel, and combed it back, tying it in a topknot.

"We'll get this cut," she muttered, and ran her hand over my face. "You don't have much beard yet. I wonder how old you are? Sixteen?"

I nodded. She shook her head and sighed. "Lord Shigeru wants you to eat with him," she said, and then added quietly, "I hope you will not bring him more grief."

I guessed Ichiro had been sharing his misgivings with her.

I followed her back to the house, trying to take in every aspect of it. It was almost dark by now; lamps in iron stands shed an orange glow in the corners of the rooms, but did not give enough light for me to see much. Chiyo led me to a staircase in the corner of the main living room. I had never seen one before: We had ladders in Mino, but no one had a proper staircase like this. The wood was dark, with a high polish— oak, I thought—and each step made its own tiny sound as I trod on it. Again, it seemed to me to be a work of magic, and I thought I could hear the voice of its creator within it.

The room was empty, the screens overlooking the garden wide open. It was just beginning to rain. Chiyo bowed to me—not very deeply, I noticed—and went back down the staircase. I listened to her footsteps and heard her speak to the maids in the kitchen.

I thought the room was the most beautiful I had ever been in. Since then I've known my share of castles, palaces, nobles' residences, but nothing can compare with the way the upstairs room in Lord Otori's house looked that evening late in the eight-month with the rain falling gently on the garden outside. At the back of the room one huge pole, the trunk of a single cedar, rose from floor to ceiling, polished to reveal the knots and the grain of the wood. The beams were of cedar, too, their soft reddish brown contrasting with the creamy white walls. The matting was already fading to soft gold, the edges joined by broad strips of indigo material with the Otori heron woven into them in white.

A scroll hung in the alcove with a painting of a small bird on it. It looked like the green-and-white-winged fly-catcher from my forest. It was so real that I half expected it to fly away. It amazed me that a great painter would have known so well the humble birds of the mountain.

I heard footsteps below and sat down quickly on the

floor, my feet tucked neatly beneath me. Through the open windows I could see a great gray and white heron standing in one of the garden pools. Its beak jabbed into the water and came up holding some little wriggling creature. The heron lifted itself elegantly upwards and flew away over the wall.

Lord Otori came into the room, followed by two of the girls carrying trays of food. He looked at me and nodded. I bowed to the floor. It occurred to me that he, Otori Shigeru, was the heron and I was the little wriggling thing he had scooped up, plunging down the mountain into my world and swooping away again.

The rain fell more heavily, and the house and garden began to sing with water. It overflowed from the gutters and ran down the chains and into the stream that leaped from pool to pool, every waterfall making a different sound. The house sang to me, and I fell in love with it. I wanted to belong to it. I would do anything for it, and anything its owner wanted me to do.

When we had finished the meal and the trays had been removed, we sat by the open window as night drew in. In the last of the light, Lord Otori pointed towards the end of the garden. The stream that cascaded through it swept under a low opening in the tiled roof wall into the river beyond. The river gave a deep, constant roar and its gray-green waters filled the opening like a painted screen.

"It's good to come home," he said quietly. "But just as the river is always at the door, so is the world always outside. And it is in the world that we have to live."

·2·

The same year Otori Shigeru rescued the boy who was to become Otori Takeo at Mino, certain events took place in a castle a long way to the south. The castle had been given to Noguchi Masayoshi by Iida Sadamu for his part in the battle of Yaegahara. Iida, having defeated his traditional enemies, the Otori, and forced their surrender on favorable terms to himself, now turned his attention to the third great clan of the Three Countries, the Seishuu, whose domains covered most of the south and west. The Seishuu preferred to make peace through alliances rather than war, and these were sealed with hostages, both from great domains, like the Maruyama, and smaller ones, like their close relatives, the Shirakawa.

Lord Shirakawa's eldest daughter, Kaede, went to Noguchi Castle as a hostage when she had just changed her sash of childhood for a girl's, and she had now lived there for half her life—long enough to think of a thousand things she detested about it. At night, when she was too tired to sleep and did not dare even toss and turn in case one of the older girls reached over and slapped her, she made lists of them inside her head. She had learned early to keep her thoughts to herself. At least no one could reach inside and slap her mind, although she knew more than one of them longed to. Which was why they slapped her so often on her body or face.

She clung with a child's single-mindedness to the faint memories she had of the home she had left when she was seven. She had not seen her mother or her younger sisters since the day her father had escorted her to the castle.

Her father had returned three times since then, only to find she was housed with the servants, not with the Noguchi children, as would have been suitable for the daughter of a warrior family. His humiliation was complete: He was unable even to protest, although she, unnaturally observant even at that age, had seen the shock and fury in his eyes. The first two times they had been allowed to speak in private for a few moments. Her clearest memory was of him holding her by the shoulders and saying in an intense voice, "If only you had been born a boy!" The third time he was permitted only to look at her. After that he had not come again, and she had had no word from her home.

She understood his reasons perfectly. By the time she was twelve, through a mixture of keeping her eyes and ears open and engaging the few people sympathetic to her in seemingly innocent conversation, she knew her own position: She was a hostage, a pawn in the struggles between the clans. Her life was worth nothing to the lords who virtually owned her, except in what she added to their bargaining power. Her father was the lord of the strategically important domain of Shirakawa; her mother was closely related to the Maruyama. Since her father had no sons, he would adopt as his heir whoever Kaede was married to. The Noguchi, by possessing her, also possessed his loyalty, his alliance, and his inheritance.

She no longer even considered the great things—fear, homesickness, loneliness—but the sense that the Noguchi did not even value her as a hostage headed her list of things she hated, as she hated the way the girls teased her for being left-handed and clumsy, the stench of the guards' room by the gate, the steep stairs that were so hard to climb when you were carrying things . . . And she was always carrying things: bowls of cold water, kettles of hot water, food for the always-ravenous men to cram into their mouths, things they had forgotten or were too lazy to fetch for themselves. She hated the castle itself, the massive stones of the foundations, the dark oppressiveness of the upper rooms, where the twisted roof beams seemed to echo her feelings, wanted to break free of the distortion they were trapped in and fly back to the forest they came from.

And the men. How she hated them. The older she grew, the more they harassed her. The maids her age competed for their attentions. They flattered and cosseted the men, putting on childish voices, pretending to be delicate, even simpleminded, to gain the protection of one soldier or another. Kaede did not blame them for it—she had come to believe that all women should use every weapon they had to protect themselves in the battle that life seemed to be—but she would not stoop to that. She could not. Her only value, her only escape from the castle, lay in marriage to someone of her own class. If she threw that chance away, she was as good as dead.

She knew she should not have to endure it. She should

go to someone and complain. Of course it was unthinkable to approach Lord Noguchi, but maybe she could ask to speak to the lady. On second thought, even to be allowed access to her seemed unlikely. The truth was, there was no one to turn to. She would have to protect herself. But the men were so strong. She was tall for a girl—too tall, the other girls said maliciously—and not weak—the hard work saw to that—but once or twice a man had grabbed her in play and held her just with one hand, and she had not been able to escape. The memory made her shiver with fear.

And every month it became harder to avoid their attentions. Late in the eighth month of her fifteenth year a typhoon in the West brought days of heavy rain. Kaede hated the rain, the way it made everything smell of mold and dampness, and she hated the way her skimpy robes clung to her when they were wet, showing the curve of her back and thighs, making the men call after her even more.

"Hey, Kaede, little sister!" a guard shouted to her as she ran through the rain from the kitchen, past the second turreted gate. "Don't go so fast! I've got an errand for you! Tell Captain Arai to come down, will you? His lordship wants him to check out a new horse."

The rain was pouring like a river from the crenellations, from the tiles, from the gutters, from the dolphins that topped every roof as a protection against fire. The whole castle spouted water. Within seconds she was soaked, her sandals saturated, making her slip and stumble on the cobbled steps. But she obeyed without too much bitterness; for, of everyone in the castle, Arai was the only person she did not hate. He always spoke nicely to her, he didn't tease or harass her, and she knew his lands lay alongside her father's and he spoke with the same slight accent of the West.

"Hey, Kaede!" The guard leered as she entered the main keep. "You're always running everywhere! Stop and chat!"

When she ignored him and started up the stairs, he shouted after her, "They say you're really a boy! Come here and show me you're not a boy!"

"Fool!" she muttered, her legs aching as she began the second flight of stairs.

The guards on the top floor were playing some kind of gambling game with a knife. Arai got to his feet as soon as he saw her and greeted her by name.

"Lady Shirakawa." He was a big man, with an impressive presence and intelligent eyes. She gave him the message. He thanked her, looking for a moment as though he would say something more to her, but seemed to change his mind. He went hastily down the stairs.

She lingered, gazing out of the windows. The wind from the mountains blew in, raw and damp. The view was almost completely blotted out by clouds, but below her was the Noguchi residence, where, she thought resentfully, she should by rights be living, not running around in the rain at everyone's beck and call.

"If you're going to dawdle, Lady Shirakawa, come and sit down with us," one of the guards said, coming up behind her and patting her on the backside.

"Get your hands off me!" she said angrily.

The men laughed. She feared their mood: They were bored and tense, fed up with the rain, the constant watching and waiting, the lack of action.

"Ah, the captain forgot his knife," one of them said. "Kaede, run down after him."

She took the knife, feeling its weight and balance in her left hand.

"She looks dangerous!" the men joked. "Don't cut yourself, little sister!"

She ran down the stairs, but Arai had already left the keep. She heard his voice in the yard and was about to call to him, but before she could get outside, the man who had spoken to her earlier stepped out of the guardroom. She stopped dead, hiding the knife behind her back. He stood right in front of her, too close, blocking the dim gray light from outside.

"Come on, Kaede, show me you're not a boy!"

He grabbed her by the right hand and pulled her close to him, pushing one leg between hers, forcing her thighs apart. She felt the hard bulge of his sex against her, and with her left hand, almost without thinking, she jabbed the knife into his neck.

He cried out instantly and let go of her, clasping his hands to his neck and staring at her with amazed eyes. He was not badly hurt, but the wound was bleeding freely. She could not believe what she had done. *I am dead*, she thought. As the man began to shout for help, Arai came back through the doorway. He took in the scene at a glance, grabbed the knife from Kaede, and without hesitation slit the guard's throat. The man fell, gurgling, to the ground.

Arai pulled Kaede outside. The rain sluiced over them.

He whispered, "He tried to rape you. I came back and killed him. Anything else and we are both dead."

She nodded. He had left his weapon behind, she had stabbed a guard: both unforgivable offenses. Arai's swift action had removed the only witness. She thought she would be shocked at the man's death and at her part in it, but she found she was only glad. *So may they all die*, she thought, *the Noguchi, the Tohan, the whole clan*.

"I will speak to his lordship on your behalf, Lady Shirakawa," Arai said, making her start with surprise. "He should not leave you unprotected." He added, almost to himself, "A man of honor would not do that."

He gave a great shout up the stairwell for the guards, then said to Kaede, "Don't forget, I saved your life. More than your life!"

She looked at him directly. "Don't forget, it was your knife," she returned.

He gave a wry smile of forced respect. "We are in each other's hands, then."

"What about them?" she said, hearing the thud of steps on the stairs. "They know I left with the knife."

"They will not betray me," he replied. "I can trust them."

"I trust no one," she whispered.

"You must trust me," he said.

Later that day Kaede was told she was to move to the Noguchi family residence. As she wrapped her few belongings into her carrying cloth, she stroked the faded pattern, with its crests of the white river for her family and the setting sun of the Seishuu. She was bitterly ashamed of how little she owned. The events of the day kept going through her mind: the feel of the knife in the forbidden left hand, the grip of the man, his lust, the way he had died. And Arai's words: *A man of honor would not do that!* He should not have spoken of his lord like that. He would never have dared to, not even to her, if he did not already have rebellion in his mind. Why had he treated her so well, not only at that vital moment, but previously? Was he, too, seeking allies? He was already a powerful and popular man; now she saw that he might have greater ambitions. He was capable of acting in an instant, seizing opportunities.

She weighed all these things carefully, knowing that even the smallest of them added to her holding in the currency of power.

All day the other girls avoided her, talking together in

huddled groups, falling silent when she passed them. Two had red eyes; perhaps the dead man had been a favorite or a lover. No one showed her any sympathy. Their resentment made her hate them more. Most of them had homes in the town or nearby villages: They had parents and families they could turn to. They were not hostages. And he, the dead guard, had grabbed her, had tried to force her. Anyone who loved such a man was an idiot.

A servant girl she had never seen before came to fetch her, addressing her as Lady Shirakawa and bowing respectfully to her. Kaede followed her down the steep cobbled steps that led from the castle to the residence, through the bailey, under the huge gate, where the guards turned their faces away from her in anger, and into the gardens that surrounded Lord Noguchi's house.

She had often seen the gardens from the castle, but this was the first time she had walked in them since she was seven years old. They went to the back of the large house, and Kaede was shown into a small room.

"Please wait here for a few minutes, lady."

After the girl had gone, Kaede knelt on the floor. The room was of good proportions, even though it was not large, and the doors stood open onto a tiny garden. The rain had stopped and the sun was shining fitfully, turning the dripping garden into a mass of shimmering light. She gazed at the stone lantern, the little twisted pine, the cistern of clear water. Crickets were singing in the branches; a frog croaked briefly. The peace and the silence melted something in her heart, and she suddenly felt near tears.

She fought them back, fixing her mind on how much she hated the Noguchi. She slipped her arms inside her sleeves and felt the bruises. She hated them all the more for living in this beautiful place, while she, of the Shirakawa family, had been housed with servants.

The internal door behind her slid open, and a woman's voice said, "Lord Noguchi wishes to speak with you, lady."

"Then you must help me get ready," she said. She could not bear to go into his presence looking as she did, her hair undressed, her clothes old and dirty.

The woman stepped into the room, and Kaede turned to look at her. She was old, and although her face was smooth and her hair still black, her hands were wrinkled and gnarled like a monkey's paws. She studied Kaede with a look of surprise on her face. Then, without speaking, she unpacked the bundle, taking out a slightly cleaner robe, a comb, and hairpins.

"Where are my lady's other clothes?"

"I came here when I was seven," Kaede said angrily. "Don't you think I might have grown since then? My mother sent better things for me, but I was not allowed to keep them!"

The woman clicked her tongue. "It's lucky that my lady's beauty is such that she has no need of adornment."

"What are you talking about?" Kaede said, for she had no idea what she looked like.

"I'll dress your hair now. And find you clean footwear. I am Junko. Lady Noguchi has sent me to wait on you. I'll speak to her later about clothes."

Junko left the room and came back with two girls carrying a bowl of water, clean socks, and a small carved box. Junko washed Kaede's face, hands and feet, and combed out her long black hair. The maids murmured as if in amazement.

"What is it? What do they mean?" Kaede said nervously.

Junko opened the box and took out a round mirror. Its back was beautifully carved with flowers and birds. She held it so Kaede could see her reflection. It was the first time she had looked in a mirror. Her own face silenced her.

The women's attentions and admiration restored her confidence a little, but it began to seep away again as she followed Junko into the main part of the residence. She had only seen Lord Noguchi from a distance since her father's last visit. She had never liked him, and now she realized she was afraid of the meeting.

Junko fell to her knees, slid open the door to the audience room, and prostrated herself. Kaede stepped into the room and did the same. The matting was cool beneath her forehead and smelled of summer grass.

Lord Noguchi was speaking to someone in the room and took no notice of her whatsoever. He seemed to be discussing his rice allowances: how late the farmers were in handing them over. It was nearly the next harvest, and he was still owed part of the last crop. Every now and then the person he was addressing would humbly put in a placatory comment—the adverse weather, last year's earthquake, the imminent typhoon season, the devotion of the farmers, the loyalty of the retainers—at which the lord would grunt, fall silent for a full minute or more, and then start complaining all over again.

Finally he fell silent for one last time. The secretary coughed once or twice. Lord Noguchi barked a command, and the secretary backed on his knees towards the door.

He passed close to Kaede, but she did not dare raise her head.

"And call Arai," Lord Noguchi said, as if it were an afterthought.

Now he will speak to me, Kaede thought, but he said nothing, and she remained where she was, motionless.

The minutes passed. She heard a man enter the room and saw Arai prostrate himself next to her. Lord Noguchi did not acknowledge him either. He clapped his hands, and several men came quickly into the room. Kaede felt them step by her, one after another. Glancing at them sideways, she could see they were senior retainers. Some wore the Noguchi crest on their robes, and some the triple oak leaf of the Tohan. She felt they would have happily stepped on her, as if she were a cockroach, and she vowed to herself that she would never let the Tohan or the Noguchi crush her.

The warriors settled themselves heavily on the matting.

"Lady Shirakawa," Lord Noguchi said at last. "Please sit up."

As she did so, she felt the eyes of every man in the room on her. An intensity that she did not understand came into the atmosphere.

"Cousin," the lord said, a note of surprise in his voice, "I hope you are well."

"Thanks to your care, I am," she replied, using the polite phrase, although the words burned her tongue like poison. She felt her terrible vulnerability here, the only woman, hardly more than a child, among men of power and brutality. She snatched a quick glance at the lord from below her lashes. His face looked petulant to her, lacking either strength or intelligence, showing the spitefulness she already knew he possessed.

"There was an unfortunate incident this morning," Lord Noguchi said. The hush in the room deepened. "Arai has told me what happened. I want to hear your version."

Kaede touched her head to the ground, her movements slow, her thoughts racing. She had Arai in her power at that moment. And Lord Noguchi had not called him captain, as he should have done. He had given him no title, shown him no courtesy. Did he already have suspicions about his loyalty? Did he already know the true version of events? Had one of the guards already betrayed Arai? If she defended him, was she just falling into a trap set for them both?

Arai was the only person in the castle who had treated her well. She was not going to betray him now. She sat up and spoke with downcast eyes but in a steady voice. "I went to the upper guardroom to give a message to Lord Arai. I followed him down the stairs: He was wanted in the stables. The guard on the gate detained me with some pretext. When I went to him he seized me." She let the sleeves fall back from her arm. The bruises had already begun to show, the purple-red imprint of a man's fingers on her pale skin. "I cried out. Lord Arai heard me, came back, and rescued me." She bowed again, conscious of her own grace. "I owe him and my lord a debt for my protection." She stayed, her head on the floor.

"Unnh," Lord Noguchi grunted. There was another long silence. Insects droned in the afternoon heat. Sweat glistened on the brows of the men sitting motionless. Kaede could smell their rank animal odor, and she felt sweat trickle between her breasts. She was intensely aware of her real danger. If one of the guards had spoken of the knife left behind, the girl who took it and walked down the stairs with it in her hand . . . she willed the thoughts away, afraid the men who studied her so closely would be able to read them clearly.

Eventually Lord Noguchi spoke, casually, even amiably. "How was the horse, Captain Arai?"

Arai raised his head to speak. His voice was perfectly calm. "Very young, but fine looking. Of excellent stock and easy to tame."

There was a ripple of amusement. Kaede felt they were laughing at her, and the blood rose in her cheeks.

"You have many talents, Captain," Noguchi said. "I am sorry to deprive myself of them, but I think your country estate, your wife and son, may need your attention for a while, a year or two. . . ."

"Lord Noguchi." Arai bowed, his face showing nothing.

What a fool Noguchi is, Kaede thought. *I'd make sure Arai stayed right here where I could keep an eye on him. Send him away and he'll be in open revolt before a year has passed.*

Arai backed out, not looking even once towards Kaede. *Noguchi's probably planning to have him murdered on the road*, she thought gloomily. *I'll never see him again.*

With Arai's departure the atmosphere lightened a little. Lord Noguchi coughed and cleared his throat. The warriors shifted position, easing their legs and backs. Kaede could feel their eyes still on her. The bruises on her arms, the man's death, had aroused them. They were no different from him.

The door behind her slid open, and the servant who had brought her from the castle came in with bowls of tea. She served each of the men and seemed to be about to leave when Lord Noguchi barked at her. She bowed, flustered, and set a cup in front of Kaede.

Kaede sat up and drank, eyes lowered, her mouth so dry she could barely swallow. Arai's punishment was exile; what would hers be?

"Lady Shirakawa, you have been with us for many years. You have been part of our household."

"You have honored me, lord," she replied.

"But I think that pleasure is to be ours no longer. I have lost two men on your account. I'm not sure I can afford to keep you with me!" He chuckled, and the men in the room laughed in echo.

He's sending me home! The false hope fluttered in her heart.

"You obviously are old enough to be married. I think the

sooner the better. We will arrange a suitable marriage for you. I am writing to inform your parents who I have in mind. You will live with my wife until the day of your marriage."

She bowed again, but before she did so, she caught the glance that flickered between Noguchi and one of the older men in the room. *It will be to him*, she thought, *or a man like him, old, depraved, brutal.* The idea of marriage to anyone appalled her. Even the thought that she would be better treated living in the Noguchi household could not raise her spirits.

Junko escorted her back to the room and then led her to the bathhouse. It was early evening and Kaede was numb with exhaustion. Junko washed her and scrubbed her back and limbs with rice bran.

"Tomorrow I will wash your hair," she promised. "It's too long and thick to wash tonight. It will never dry in time, and then you will take a chill."

"Maybe I will die from it," Kaede said. "It would be the best thing."

"Never say that," Junko scolded her, helping her into the tub to soak in the hot water. "You have a great life ahead of you. You are so beautiful! You will be married, have children."

She brought her mouth close to Kaede's ear and whispered, "The captain thanks you for keeping faith with him. I am to look after you on his behalf."

What can women do in this world of men? Kaede thought. *What protection do we have? Can anyone look after me?*

She remembered her own face in the mirror, and longed to look at it again.

· 3 ·

The heron came to the garden every afternoon, floating like a gray ghost over the wall, folding itself improbably, and standing thigh deep in the pool, as still as a statue of Jizo. The red and gold carp that Lord Otori took pleasure in feeding were too large for it, but it held its position motionless for long minutes at a time, until some hapless creature forgot it was there and dared to move in the water. Then the heron struck, faster than eye could follow, and, with the little wriggling thing in its beak, reassembled itself for flight. The first few wing beats were as loud as the sudden clacking of a fan, but after that it departed as silently as it had come.

The days were still very hot, with the languorous heat of autumn, which you long to be over and cling on to at the same time, knowing this fiercest heat, hardest to bear, will also be the year's last.

I had been in Lord Otori's house for a month. In Hagi the rice harvest was over, the straw drying in the fields and on frames around the farmhouses. The red autumn lilies were fading. Persimmons turned gold on the trees while the leaves became brittle, and spiny chestnut shells lay in the lanes and alleys, spilling out their glossy fruit. The autumn full moon came and went. Chiyo put chestnuts, tangerines, and rice cakes in the garden shrine, and I wondered if anyone was doing the same in my village.

The servant girls gathered the last of the wildflowers, bush clover, wild pinks, and autumn wort, standing them in buckets outside the kitchen and the privy, their fragrance masking the smells of food and waste, the cycles of human life.

My state of half-being, my speechlessness, persisted. I suppose I was in mourning. The Otori household was, too, not only for Lord Otori's brother but also for his mother, who had died in the summer from the plague. Chiyo related the story of the family to me. Shigeru, the oldest son, had been with his father at the battle of Yaegahara and had strongly opposed the surrender to the Tohan. The terms of the surrender had forbidden him inheriting from his father the leadership of the clan. Instead his uncles, Shoichi and Masahiro, were appointed by Iida.

"Iida Sadamu hates Shigeru more than any man alive," Chiyo said. "He is jealous of him and fears him."

Shigeru was a thorn in the side of his uncles as well, as the legal heir to the clan. He had ostensibly withdrawn from the political stage and had devoted himself to his land, trying out new methods, experimenting with different crops. He had married young, but his wife had died two years later in childbirth, the baby dying with her.

His life seemed to me to be filled with suffering, yet he gave no sign of it, and if I had not learned all this from Chiyo I would not have known of it. I spent most of the day with him, following him around like a dog, always at his side, except when I was studying with Ichiro.

They were days of waiting. Ichiro tried to teach me to read and write, my general lack of skill and retentiveness enraging him, while he reluctantly pursued the idea of adoption. The clan were opposed: Lord Shigeru should marry again, he was still young, it was too soon after his mother's death. The objections seemed to be endless. I could not help feeling that Ichiro agreed with most of them, and they seemed perfectly valid to me too. I tried my hardest to learn, because I did not want to disappoint the lord, but I had no real belief or trust in my situation.

Usually in the late afternoon Lord Shigeru would send for me, and we would sit by the window and look at the garden. He did not say much, but he would study me when he thought I was not looking. I felt he was waiting for something: for me to speak, for me to give some sign—but of what I did not know. It made me anxious, and the anxiety made me more sure that I was disappointing him and even less able to learn. One afternoon Ichiro came to the upper room to complain again about me. He had been exasperated to the point of beating me earlier that day. I was sulking in the corner, nursing my bruises, tracing with my finger on the matting the shapes of the characters I'd learned that day, in a desperate attempt to try to retain them.

"You made a mistake," Ichiro said. "No one will think the worse of you if you admit it. The circumstances of your brother's death explain it. Send the boy back to where he came from, and get on with your life."

And let me get on with mine, I felt he was saying. He never let me forget the sacrifices he was making in trying to educate me.

"You can't re-create Lord Takeshi," he added, softening his tone a little. "He was the result of years of education and training—and the best blood to begin with."

I was afraid Ichiro would get his way. Lord Shigeru was as bound to him and Chiyo by the ties and obligations of duty as they were to him. I'd thought he had all the power in the household, but in fact Ichiro had his own power, and knew how to wield it. And in the opposite direction, his uncles had power over Lord Shigeru. He had to obey the dictates of the clan. There was no reason for him to keep me, and he would never be allowed to adopt me.

"Watch the heron, Ichiro," Lord Shigeru said. "You see his patience, you see how long he stands without moving to get what he needs. I have the same patience, and it's far from exhausted."

Ichiro's lips were pressed tight together in his favorite sour-plum expression. At that moment the heron stabbed and left, clacking its wings.

I could hear the squeaking that heralded the evening

arrival of the bats. I lifted my head to see two of them swoop into the garden. While Ichiro continued to grumble, and the lord to answer him briefly, never losing his temper, I listened to the noises of the approaching night. Every day my hearing grew sharper. I was becoming used to it, learning to filter out whatever I did not need to listen to, giving no sign that I could hear everything that went on in the house. No one knew that I could hear all their secrets.

Now I heard the hiss of hot water as the bath was prepared, the clatter of dishes from the kitchen, the sliding sigh of the cook's knife, the tread of a girl in soft socks on the boards outside, the stamp and whinny of a horse in the stables, the cry of the female cat, feeding four kittens and always famished, a dog barking two streets away, the clack of clogs over the wooden bridges of the canals, children singing, the temple bells from Tokoji and Daishoin. I knew the song of the house, day and night, in sunshine and under the rain. This evening I realized I was always listening for something more. I was waiting too. For what? Every night before I fell asleep my mind replayed the scene on the mountain, the severed head, the wolf man clutching the stump of his arm. I saw again Iida Sadamu on the ground, and the bodies of my stepfather and Isao. Was I waiting for Iida and the wolf man to catch up with me? Or for my chance of revenge?

From time to time I still tried to pray in the manner of the Hidden, and that night I prayed to be shown the path I should take. I could not sleep. The air was heavy and still, the moon, a week past full, hidden behind thick banks of cloud. The insects of the night were noisy and restless. I could hear the suck of the gecko's feet as it crossed the ceiling hunting them. Ichiro and Lord Shigeru were both sound asleep, Ichiro snoring. I did not want to leave the house I'd come to love so much, but I seemed to be bringing nothing but trouble to it. Perhaps it would be better for everyone if I just vanished in the night.

Without any real plan to go—What would I do? How would I live?—I began to wonder if I could get out of the house without setting the dogs barking and arousing the guards. That was when I started consciously listening for the dogs. Usually I heard them bark on and off throughout the night, but I'd learned to distinguish their barks and to ignore them mostly. I set my ears for them but heard nothing. Then I started listening for the guards: the sound of a foot on stone, the clink of steel, a whispered conversation. Nothing.

Sounds that should have been there were missing from the night's familiar web.

Now I was wide-awake, straining my ears to hear above the water from the garden. The stream and river were low: There had been no rain since the turn of the moon.

There came the slightest of sounds, hardly more than a tremor, between the window and the ground.

For a moment I thought it was the earth shaking, as it so often did in the Middle Country. Another tiny tremble followed, then another.

Someone was climbing up the side of the house.

My first instinct was to yell out, but cunning took over. To shout would raise the household, but it would also alert the intruder. I rose from the mattress and crept silently to Lord Shigeru's side. My feet knew the floor, knew every creak the old house would make. I knelt beside him and, as though I had never lost the power of speech, whispered in his ear, "Lord Otori, someone is outside."

He woke instantly, stared at me for a moment, then reached for the sword and knife that lay beside him. I gestured to the window. The faint tremor came again, just the slightest shifting of weight against the side of the house.

Lord Shigeru passed the knife to me and stepped to the wall. He smiled at me and pointed, and I moved to the other side of the window. We waited for the assassin to climb in.

Step-by-step he came up the wall, stealthy and unhurried, as if he had all the time in the world, confident that there was nothing to betray him. We waited for him with the same patience, almost as if we were boys playing a game in a barn.

Except the end was no game. He paused on the sill to take out the garrote he planned to use on us, and then stepped inside. Lord Shigeru took him in a stranglehold. Slippery as an eel, the intruder wriggled backwards. I leaped at him, but before I could say knife, let alone use it, the three of us fell into the garden like a flurry of fighting cats.

The man fell first, across the stream, striking his head on a boulder. Lord Shigeru landed on his feet. My fall was broken by one of the shrubs. Winded, I dropped the knife. I scrabbled to pick it up, but it was not needed. The intruder groaned, tried to rise, but slipped back into the water. His body dammed the stream; it deepened around him, then with a sudden babble flowed over him. Lord Shigeru pulled him from the water, striking him in the face and shouting at him, "Who? Who paid you? Where are you from?"

The man merely groaned again, his breath coming in loud, rasping snores.

"Get a light," Lord Shigeru said to me. I thought the household would be awake by now, but the skirmish had happened so quickly and silently that they all slept on. Dripping water and leaves, I ran to the maids' room.

"Chiyo!" I called. "Bring lights, wake the men!"

"Who's that?" she replied sleepily, not knowing my voice.

"It's me, Takeo! Wake up! Someone tried to kill Lord Shigeru!"

I took a light that still burned in one of the candle stands and carried it back to the garden.

The man had slipped further into unconsciousness. Lord Shigeru stood staring down at him. I held the light over him. The intruder was dressed in black, with no crest or marking on his clothes. He was of medium height and build, his hair cut short. There was nothing to distinguish him.

Behind us we heard the clamor of the household coming awake, screams as two guards were discovered garroted, three dogs poisoned.

Ichiro came out, pale and shaking. "Who would dare do

this?" he said. "In your own house, in the heart of Hagi? It's an insult to the whole clan!"

"Unless the clan ordered it," Lord Shigeru replied quietly.

"It's more likely to be Iida," Ichiro said. He saw the knife in my hand and took it from me. He slashed the black cloth from neck to waist, exposing the man's back. There was a hideous scar from an old sword wound across the shoulder blade, and the backbone was tattooed in a delicate pattern. It flickered like a snake in the lamplight.

"He's a hired assassin," Lord Shigeru said, "from the Tribe. He could have been paid by anyone."

"Then it must be Iida! He must know you have the boy! Now will you get rid of him?"

"If it hadn't been for the boy, the assassin would have succeeded," the lord replied. "It was he who woke me in time. . . . He spoke to me," he cried as realization dawned. "He spoke in my ear and woke me up!"

Ichiro was not particularly impressed by this. "Has it occurred to you that he might have been the target, not you?"

"Lord Otori," I said, my voice thick and husky from weeks of disuse. "I've brought nothing but danger to you. Let me go, send me away." But even as I spoke, I knew he would not. I had saved his life now, as he had saved mine, and the bond between us was stronger than ever.

Ichiro was nodding in agreement, but Chiyo spoke up: "Forgive me, Lord Shigeru. I know it's nothing to do with me and that I'm just a foolish old woman. But it's not true that Takeo has brought you nothing but danger. Before you returned with him, you were half crazed with sorrow. Now you are recovered. He has brought joy and hope as well as danger. And who dares enjoy one and escape the other?"

"How should I of all people not know this?" Lord Shigeru replied. "There is some destiny that binds our lives together. I cannot fight that, Ichiro."

"Maybe his brains will have returned with his tongue," Ichiro said scathingly.

The assassin died without regaining consciousness. It turned out he'd had a poison pellet in his mouth and had crushed it as he fell. No one knew his identity, though there were plenty of rumors. The dead guards were buried in a solemn ceremony, and mourned, and the dogs were mourned by me, at least. I wondered what pact they had made, what fealty they had sworn, to be caught up in the feuds of men, and to pay with their lives. I did not voice these thoughts: There were plenty more dogs. New ones were acquired and trained to take food from one man only so they could not be poisoned. There were any number of men, too, for that matter. Lord Shigeru lived simply, with few armed retainers, but it seemed many among the Otori clan would have happily come to serve him—enough to form an army, if he'd so desired.

The attack did not seem to have alarmed or depressed him in any way. If anything, he was invigorated by it, his delight in the pleasures of life sharpened by his escape from death. He floated, as he had done after the meeting with Lady Maruyama. He was delighted by my newly recovered speech and by the sharpness of my hearing.

Maybe Ichiro was right, or maybe his own attitude towards me softened. Whatever the reason, from the night of the assassination attempt on, learning became easier. Slowly the characters began to unlock their meaning and retain their place in my brain. I even began to enjoy them, the different shapes that flowed like water, or perched solid and squat like black crows in winter. I wouldn't admit it to Ichiro, but drawing them gave me a deep pleasure.

Ichiro was an acknowledged master, well known for the beauty of his writing and the depth of his learning. He was really far too good a teacher for me. I did not have the mind of a natural student. But what we both discovered was that I could mimic. I could present a passable copy of a student, just as I could copy the way he'd draw from the shoulder, not the wrist, with boldness and concentration. I knew I was just mimicking him, but the results were adequate.

The same thing happened when Lord Shigeru taught me the use of the sword. I was strong and agile enough, probably more than average for my height, but I had missed the boyhood years when the sons of warriors practice endlessly at sword, bow, and horsemanship. I knew I would never make them up.

Riding came easily enough. I watched Lord Shigeru and the other men, and realized it was mainly a matter of balance. I simply copied what I saw them do and the horse responded. I realized, too, that the horse was shyer and more nervous than I was. To the horse I had to act like a lord, hide my own feelings for his sake, and pretend I was perfectly in control and knew exactly what was going on. Then the horse would relax beneath me and be happy.

I was given a pale gray horse with a black mane and tail, called Raku, and we got on well together. I did not take to archery at all, but in using the sword again I copied what I saw Lord Shigeru do, and the results were passable. I was given a long sword of my own, and wore it in the sash of my new clothes as any warrior's son would. But despite the sword and the clothes I knew I was only an imitation warrior.

So the weeks went by. The household accepted that Lord Otori intended to adopt me, and little by little their attitude towards me changed. They spoiled, teased, and scolded me in equal measures. Between the studying and training I had little spare time and I was not supposed to go out alone, but I still had my restless love of roaming, and whenever I could I slipped away and explored the city of Hagi. I liked to go down to the port, where the castle in the West and the old volcano crater in the East held the bay like a cup in their two hands. I'd stare out to sea and think of all the fabled lands that lay beyond the horizon and envy the sailors and fishermen.

There was one boat that I always looked for. A boy about my own age worked on it. I knew he was called Terada Fumio. His father was from a low-rank warrior family who had taken up trade and fishing rather than die of starvation. Chiyo knew all about them, and I got this information at first from her. I admired Fumio enormously. He had actually been to the mainland. He knew the sea and the rivers in all their moods. At that time I could not even swim. At first we just nodded at each other, but as the weeks went by we became friends. I'd go aboard and we'd sit and eat persimmons, spitting the pips into the water, and talk about the things boys talk about. Sooner or later we would get on to the Otori lords; the Terada hated them for their arrogance and greed. They suffered from the ever-increasing taxes that the castle imposed, and from the restrictions placed on trade. When we talked about these things it was in whispers, on the seaward side of the boat, for the castle, it was said, had spies everywhere.

I was hurrying home late one afternoon after one of these excursions. Ichiro had been called to settle an account with a merchant. I'd waited for ten minutes and then decided he was not coming back and made my escape. It was well into the tenth month. The air was cool and filled with the smell of burning rice straw. The smoke hung over the fields between the river and the mountains, turning the landscape silver and gold. Fumio had been teaching me to swim, and my hair was wet, making me shiver a little. I was thinking about hot water and wondering if I could get something to eat from Chiyo before the evening meal, and whether Ichiro would be in a bad enough temper to beat me, and at the same time I was listening, as I always did, for the moment when I would begin to hear the distinct song of the house from the street.

I thought I heard something else, something that made me stop and look twice at the corner of the wall, just before our gate. I did not think there was anyone there, then almost in the same instant I saw there was someone, a man squatting on his heels in the shadow of the tile roof.

I was only a few yards from him, on the opposite side of the street. I knew he'd seen me. After a few moments he stood up slowly as if waiting for me to approach him.

He was the most ordinary-looking person I'd ever seen, average height and build, hair going a little gray, face pale rather than brown, with unmemorable features, the sort that you can never be sure of recognizing again. Even as I studied him, trying to work him out, his features seemed to change shape before my eyes. And yet, beneath the very ordinariness lay something extraordinary, something deft and quick that slipped away when I tried to pinpoint it.

He was wearing faded blue-gray clothes and carrying no visible weapon. He did not look like a workman, a merchant, or a warrior. I could not place him in any way, but some inner sense warned me that he was very dangerous.

At the same time there was something about him that fascinated me. I could not pass by without acknowledging him. But I stayed on the far side of the street, and was already judging how far it was to the gate, the guards, and the dogs.

He gave me a nod and a smile, almost of approval. "Good day, young lord!" he called, in a voice that held mockery just below the surface. "You're right not to trust me. I've heard you're clever like that. But I'll never harm you, I promise you."

I felt his speech was as slippery as his appearance, and I did not count his promise for much.

"I want to talk to you," he said, "and to Shigeru too."

I was astonished to hear him speak of the lord in that familiar way. "What do you have to say to me?"

"I can't shout it to you from here," he replied with a laugh. "Walk with me to the gate and I'll tell you."

"You can walk to the gate on that side of the road and I'll walk on this side," I said, watching his hands to catch the first movement towards a hidden weapon. "Then I'll speak to Lord Otori and he can decide if you are to meet him or not."

The man smiled to himself and shrugged, and we walked separately to the gate, he as calmly as if he were taking an evening stroll, me as jumpy as a cat before a storm. When we got to the gate and the guards greeted us, he seemed to have grown older and more faded. He looked like such a harmless old man, I was almost ashamed of my mistrust.

"You're in trouble, Takeo," one of the men said. "Master Ichiro has been looking for you for an hour!"

"Hey, Grandpa," the other called to the old man. "What are you after, a bowl of noodles or something?"

Indeed, the old man did look as if he needed a square meal. He waited humbly, saying nothing, just outside the gate sill.

"Where'd you pick him up, Takeo? You're too softhearted, that's your trouble! Get rid of him!"

"I said I would tell Lord Otori he was here, and I will," I replied. "But watch his every movement, and whatever you do, don't let him into the garden."

I turned to the stranger to say "Wait here" and caught a flash of something from him. He was dangerous, all right, but it was almost as if he were letting me see a side of him that he kept hidden from the guards. I wondered if I should leave him with them. Still, there were two of them armed to the teeth. They should be able to deal with one old man.

I tore through the garden, kicked off my sandals, and climbed the stairs in a couple of bounds. Lord Shigeru was sitting in the upstairs room, gazing out over the garden.

"Takeo," he said, "I've been thinking, a tea room over the garden would be perfect."

"Lord . . ." I began, then was transfixed by a movement in the garden below. I thought it was the heron, it stood so still and gray, then I saw it was the man I had left at the gate.

"What?" Lord Shigeru said, seeing my face.

I was gripped by terror that the assassination attempt was to be repeated. "There's a stranger in the garden," I cried. "Watch him!" My next fear was for the guards. I ran back down the stairs and out of the house. My heart was pounding as I came to the gate. The dogs were all right. They stirred when they heard me, tails wagging. I shouted; the men came out, astonished.

"What's wrong, Takeo?"

"'You let him in!' I said in a fury. "The old man, he's in the garden."

"No, he's out there in the street where you left him."

My eyes followed the man's gesture, and for a moment I, too, was fooled. I did see him, sitting outside in the shade of the roofed wall, humble, patient, harmless. Then my vision cleared. The street was empty.

"You fools!" I said. "Didn't I tell you he was dangerous? Didn't I tell you on no account to let him in? What useless idiots are you, and you call yourselves men of the Otori clan? Go back to your farms and guard your hens, and may the foxes eat every one of them!"

They gaped at me. I don't think any one in the household had ever heard me speak so many words at once. My rage was greater because I felt responsible for them. But they had to obey me. I could only protect them if they obeyed me.

"You are lucky to be alive," I said, drawing my sword from my belt and racing back to find the intruder.

He was gone from the garden, and I was beginning to wonder if I'd seen another mirage, when I heard voices from the upstairs room. Lord Shigeru called my name. He did not sound in any danger—more as if he were laughing. When I went into the room and bowed, the man was sitting next to him as if they were old friends, and they were both chuckling away. The stranger no longer looked so ancient. I could see he was a few years older than Lord Shigeru, and his face now was open and warm.

"He wouldn't walk on the same side of the street, eh?" the lord said.

"That's right, and he made me sit outside and wait." They both roared with laughter and slapped the matting with open palms. "By the way, Shigeru, you should train your guards better. Takeo was right to be angry with them."

"He was right all along," Lord Shigeru said, a note of pride in his voice.

"He's one in a thousand—the sort that's born, not made. He has to be from the Tribe. Sit up, Takeo, let me look at you."

I lifted my head from the floor and sat back on my heels. My face was burning. I felt the man had tricked me after all. He said nothing, just studied me quietly.

Lord Shigeru said, "This is Muto Kenji, an old friend of mine."

"Lord Muto," I said, polite but cold, determined not to let my feelings show.

"You don't have to call me lord," Kenji said. "I am not a lord, though I number a few among my friends." He leaned towards me. "Show me your hands."

He took each hand in turn, looking at the back and then at the palm.

"We think him like Takeshi," Lord Shigeru said.

"Unnh. He has a look of the Otori about him." Kenji moved back to his original position and gazed over the garden. The last of the color had leached from it. Only the maples still glowed red. "The news of your loss saddened me," he said.

"I thought I no longer wanted to live," Lord Shigeru replied. "But the weeks pass and I find that I do. I am not made for despair."

"No, indeed," Kenji agreed, with affection. They both looked out through the open windows. The air was chill with autumn, a gust of wind shook the maples, and leaves fell into the stream, turning darker red in the water before they were swept into the river.

I thought longingly of the hot bath, and shivered.

Kenji broke the silence. "Why is this boy who looks like Takeshi, but is obviously from the Tribe, living in your household, Shigeru?"

"Why have you come all this way to ask me?" he replied, smiling slightly.

"I don't mind telling you. News on the wind was that someone heard an intruder climbing into your house. As a result, one of the most dangerous assassins in the Three Countries is dead."

"We have tried to keep it secret," Lord Shigeru said.

"It's our business to find out such secrets. What was Shintaro doing in your house?"

"Presumably he came to kill me," Lord Shigeru replied. "So it was Shintaro. I had my suspicions, but we had no proof." After a moment he added, "Someone must truly desire my death. Was he hired by Iida?"

"He had worked for the Tohan for some time. But I don't think Iida would have you assassinated in secret. By all accounts he would rather watch the event with his own eyes. Who else wants you dead?"

"I can think of one or two," the lord answered.

"It was hard to believe Shintaro failed," Kenji went on.

"We had to find out who the boy was. Where did you find him?"

"What do you hear on the wind?" Lord Shigeru countered, still smiling.

"The official story, of course: that he's a distant relative of your mother's; from the superstitious, that you took leave of your senses and believe he's your brother returned to you; from the cynical, that he's your son, got with some peasant woman in the East."

Lord Shigeru laughed. "I am not even twice his age. I would have had to have fathered him at twelve. He is not my son."

"No, obviously, and despite his looks, I don't believe he's a relative or a revenant. Anyway, he has to be from the Tribe. Where did you find him?"

One of the maids, Haruka, came and lit the lamps, and immediately a large blue-green moon moth blundered into the room and flapped towards the flame. I stood and took it in my hand, felt its powdery wings beat against my palm, and released it into the night, sliding the screens closed before I sat again.

Lord Shigeru made no reply to Kenji, and then Haruka

returned with tea. Kenji did not seem angry or frustrated. He admired the tea bowls, which were of the simple, pink-hued local ware, and drank without saying any more, but watching me all the time.

Finally he asked me a direct question. "Tell me, Takeo, when you were a child, did you pull the shells off living snails, or tear the claws from crabs?"

I didn't understand the question. "Maybe," I said, pretending to drink, even though my bowl was empty.

"Did you?"

"No."

"Why not?"

"My mother told me it was cruel."

"I thought so." His voice had taken on a note of sadness, as though he pitied me. "No wonder you've been trying to fend me off, Shigeru. I felt a softness in the boy, an aversion to cruelty. He was raised among the Hidden."

"Is it so obvious?" Lord Shigeru said.

"Only to me." Kenji sat cross-legged, eyes narrowed, one arm resting on his knee. "I think I know who he is."

Lord Shigeru sighed, and his face became still and wary. "Then, you had better tell us."

"He has all the signs of being Kikuta: the long fingers, the straight line across the palm, the acute hearing. It comes on suddenly, around puberty, sometimes accompanied by loss of speech, usually temporary, sometimes permanent. . . ."

"You're making this up!" I said, unable to keep silent any longer. In fact, a sort of horror was creeping over me. I knew nothing of the Tribe, except that the assassin had been one of them, but I felt as if Muto Kenji were opening a dark door before me that I dreaded entering.

Lord Shigeru shook his head. "Let him speak. It is of great importance."

Kenji leaned forward and spoke directly to me. "I am going to tell you about your father."

Lord Shigeru said dryly, "You had better start with the Tribe. Takeo does not know what you mean when you say he is obviously Kikuta."

"Is that so?" Kenji raised one eyebrow. "Well, I suppose if he was brought up by the Hidden, I shouldn't be surprised. I'll begin at the beginning. The five families of the Tribe have always existed. They were there before the lords and the clans. They go back to a time when magic was greater than strength of arms, and the gods still walked the earth. When the clans sprang up, and men formed allegiances based on might, the Tribe did not join any of them. To preserve their gifts, they took to the roads and became travelers, actors and acrobats, peddlers and magicians."

"They may have done so in the beginning," Lord Shigeru interrupted. "But many also became merchants, amassing considerable wealth and influence." He said to me, "Kenji himself runs a very successful business in soybean products as well as money lending."

"Times have become corrupt," Kenji said. "As the priests tell us, we are in the last days of the law. I was talking about an earlier age. These days it's true, we are involved in business. From time to time we may serve one or other of the clans and take its crest, or work for those who have befriended us, like Lord Otori Shigeru. But whatever we have become, we preserve the talents from the past, which once all men had but have now forgotten."

"You were in two places at once," I said. "The guards saw you outside while I saw you in the garden."

Kenji bowed ironically to me. "We can split ourselves and leave the second self behind. We can become invisible and move faster than the eye can follow. Acuteness of vision and hearing are other traits. The Tribe has retained these abilities through dedication and hard training. And they are abilities that others in this warring country find useful, and pay highly for. Most members of the Tribe become spies or assassins at some stage in their life."

I was concentrating on trying not to shiver. My blood seemed to have drained out of me. I remembered how I had seemed to split in half beneath Iida's sword. And all the sounds of the house, the garden, and the city beyond rang with increasing intensity in my ears.

"Kikuta Isamu, who I believe was your father, was no exception. His parents were cousins and he combined the strongest gifts of the Kikuta. By the time he was thirty, he was a flawless assassin. No one knows how many he killed; most of the deaths seemed natural and were never attributed to him. Even by the standards of the Kikuta he was secretive. He was a master of poisons, in particular certain mountain plants that kill while leaving no trace.

"He was in the mountains of the East—you know the district I mean—seeking new plants. The men in the village where he was lodging were Hidden. It seems they told him about the secret god, the command not to kill, the judgment that awaits in the afterlife: You know it all, I don't need to tell you. In those remote mountains, far from the feuds of the clans, Isamu had been taking stock of his life. Perhaps he was filled with remorse. Perhaps the dead called out to him. Anyway, he renounced his life with the Tribe and became one of the Hidden."

"And was executed?" Lord Shigeru spoke out of the gloom.

"Well, he broke the fundamental rules of the Tribe. We don't like being renounced like that, especially not by someone with such great talents. That sort of ability is all too rare these days. But to tell the truth, I don't know what exactly happened to him. I didn't even know he had had a child. Takeo, or whatever his real name is, must have been born after his father's death."

"Who killed him?" I said, my mouth dry.

"Who knows? There were many who wanted to, and one of them did. Of course, no one could have got near him if he had not taken a vow never to kill again."

There was a long silence. Apart from a small pool of light from the glowing lamp, it was almost completely dark in the room. I could not see their faces, though I was sure Kenji could see mine.

"Did your mother never tell you this?" he asked eventually.

I shook my head. There is so much that the Hidden don't tell, so much they keep secret even from each other. What isn't known can't be revealed under torture. If you don't know your brother's secrets, you cannot betray him.

Kenji laughed. "Admit it, Shigeru, you had no idea who you were bringing into your household. Not even the Tribe knew of his existence—a boy with all the latent talent of the Kikuta!"

Lord Shigeru did not reply, but as he leaned forward into the lamplight I could see he was smiling, cheerful and open-hearted. I thought what a contrast there was between the two men: the lord so open, Kenji so devious and tricky.

"I need to know how this came about. I'm not talking idly with you, Shigeru. I need to know." Kenji's voice was insistent.

I could hear Chiyo fussing on the stairs. Lord Shigeru said, "We must bathe and eat. After the meal we'll talk again."

He will not want me in his house, now that he knows I am the son of an assassin. This was the first thought that came to me as I sat in the hot water, after the older men had bathed. I could hear their voices from the upper room. They were drinking wine now and reminiscing idly about the past. Then I thought about the father I had never known, and felt a deep sadness that he had not been able to escape his background. He had wanted to give up the killing, but it would not give him up. It had reached out its long arms and found him, as far away as Mino, just as, years later, Iida had sought out the Hidden there. I looked at my own long fingers. Was that what they were designed for? To kill?

Whatever I had inherited from him, I was also my mother's child. I was woven from two strands that could hardly be less alike, and both called to me through blood, muscle, and bone. I remembered, too, my fury at the guards. I knew I had been acting then as their lord. Was this to be a third strand in my life, or would I be sent away now that Lord Shigeru knew who I was?

The thoughts became too painful, too difficult to unravel, and anyway, Chiyo was calling to me to come and eat. The water had warmed me at last, and I was hungry.

Ichiro had joined Lord Shigeru and Kenji, and the trays were already set out before them. They were discussing trivial things when I arrived: the weather, the design of the garden, my poor learning skills and generally bad behavior. Ichiro was still displeased with me for disappearing that afternoon. It seemed like weeks ago that I had swum in the freezing autumn river with Fumio.

The food was even better than usual, but only Ichiro enjoyed it. Kenji ate fast, the lord hardly touched anything. I was alternately hungry and nauseated, both dreading and longing for the end of the meal. Ichiro ate so much and so slowly that I thought he would never be through. Twice we seemed to be finished when he took "Just another tiny mouthful." At last he patted his stomach and belched quietly. He was about to embark on another long gardening discussion, but Lord Shigeru made a sign to him. With a few parting comments and a couple more jokes to Kenji about me, he withdrew. Haruka and Chiyo came to clear away the dishes. When they had left, their footsteps and voices fading away to the kitchen, Kenji sat forward, his hand held out, palm open, towards Lord Shigeru.

"Well?" he said.

I wished I could follow the women. I didn't want to be sitting here while these men decided my fate. For that was what it would come to, I was sure. Kenji must have come to claim me in some way for the Tribe. And Lord Shigeru would surely be only too happy now to let me go.

"I don't know why this information is so important to you, Kenji," Lord Shigeru said. "I find it hard to believe that you don't know it all already. If I tell you, I trust it will go no further. Even in this house no one knows but Ichiro and Chiyo.

"You were right when you said I did not know whom I had brought into my house. It all happened by chance. It was late in the afternoon, I had strayed somewhat out of my path and was hoping to find lodging for the night in the village that I later discovered was called Mino. I had been traveling alone for some weeks after Takeshi's death."

"You were seeking revenge?" Kenji asked quietly.

"You know how things are between Iida and myself— how they have been since Yaegahara. But I could hardly have hoped to come upon him in that isolated place. It was purely the strangest of coincidences that we two, the most bitter enemies, should have been there on the same day. Certainly if I had met Iida there, I would have sought to kill him. But this boy ran into me on the path instead."

He briefly told of the massacre, Iida's fall from the horse, the men pursuing me.

"It happened on the spur of the moment. The men

threatened me. They were armed. I defended myself."

"Did they know who you were?"

"Probably not. I was in traveling clothes, unmarked; it was getting dark, raining."

"But you knew they were Tohan?"

"They told me Iida was after the boy. That was enough to make me want to protect him."

Kenji said, as though changing the subject, "I've heard Iida is seeking a formal alliance with the Otori."

"It's true. My uncles are in favor of making peace, although the clan itself is divided."

"If Iida learns you have the boy, the alliance will never go forward."

"There is no need to tell me things I already know," the lord said with the first flash of anger.

"Lord Otori," Kenji said in his ironic way, and bowed.

For a few moments no one spoke. Then Kenji sighed. "Well, the fates decide our lives, no matter what we think we are planning. Whoever sent Shintaro against you, the result is the same. Within a week the Tribe knew of Takeo's existence. I have to tell you that we have an interest in this boy, which we will not relinquish."

I said, my voice sounding thin in my own ears, "Lord Otori saved my life and I will not leave him."

He reached out and patted me on the shoulder as a father might. "I'm not giving him up," he said to Kenji.

"We want above all to keep him alive," Kenji replied. "While it seems safe, he can stay here. There is one other concern, though. The Tohan you met on the mountain: Presumably you killed them?"

"One at least," Lord Shigeru replied, "possibly two."

"One," Kenji corrected him.

Lord Shigeru raised his eyebrows. "You know all the answers already. Why do you bother asking?"

"I need to fill in certain gaps, and know how much you know."

"One, two—what does it matter?"

"The man who lost his arm survived. His name is Ando; he's long been one of Iida's closest men."

I remembered the wolfish man who had pursued me up the path, and could not help shivering.

"He did not know who you were, and does not yet know where Takeo is. But he is looking for you both. With Iida's permission, he has devoted himself to the quest for revenge."

"I look forward to our next meeting," Lord Shigeru replied.

Kenji stood and paced around the room. When he sat down, his face was open and smiling, as though we had done nothing all evening save exchange jokes and talk about gardens.

"It's good," he said. "Now that I know exactly what danger Takeo is in, I can set about protecting him and teaching him to protect himself." Then he did something that astonished me: He bowed to the floor before me and said, "While I am alive, you will be safe. I swear it to you." I thought he was being ironic, but some disguise slipped from his face, and for a moment I saw the true man beneath. I might have seen Jato come alive. Then the cover slipped back, and Kenji was joking again. "But you have to do exactly what I tell you!"

He grinned at me. "I gather Ichiro finds you too much. He shouldn't be bothered by cubs like you at his age. I will take over your education. I will be your teacher."

He drew his robe around him with a fussy movement and pursed his lips, instantly becoming the gentle old man I had left outside the gate. "That is, if Lord Otori will graciously permit it."

"I don't seem to have any choice," Lord Shigeru said, and poured more wine, smiling his openhearted smile.

My eyes flicked from one face to the other. Again I was struck by the contrast between them. I thought I saw in Kenji's eyes a look that was not quite scorn, but close to it. Now that I know the ways of the Tribe so intimately, I know their weakness is arrogance. They become infatuated with their own amazing skills, and underestimate those of their antagonists. But at that moment Kenji's look just angered me.

Shortly after that, the maids came to spread out the beds and put out the lamps. For a long time I lay sleepless, listening to the sounds of the night. The evening's revelations marched slowly through my mind, scattered, re-formed, and marched past again. My life no longer belonged to me. But for Lord Shigeru I would be dead now. If he had not run into me by accident, as he said, on the mountain path . . .

Was it really by accident? Everyone, even Kenji, accepted his version: It had all happened on the spur of the moment, the running boy, the threatening men, the fight . . .

I relived it all in my mind. And I seemed to recall a moment when the path ahead was clear. There was a huge tree, a cedar, and someone stepped out from behind it and seized me—not by accident, but deliberately. I thought of Lord Shigeru and how little I really knew about him. Everyone took him at face value: impulsive, warmhearted, generous. I believed him to be all these things, but I couldn't help wondering what lay beneath. *I'm not giving him up*, he had said. But why would he want to adopt one of the Tribe, the son of an assassin? I thought of the heron, and how patiently it waited before it struck.

The sky was lightening and the roosters were crowing before I slept.

The guards had a lot of fun at my expense when Muto Kenji was installed as my teacher.

"Watch out for the old man, Takeo! He's pretty dangerous. He might stab you with the brush!"

It was a joke they never seemed to tire of. I learned to say nothing. Better they should think me an idiot than that they should know and spread abroad the old man's real identity. It was an early lesson for me. The less people think of you, the more they will reveal to you or in your presence. I began to wonder how many blank-faced, seemingly dull-witted but trustworthy servants or retainers were really from the Tribe, carrying out their work of intrigue, subterfuge, and sudden death.

Kenji initiated me into the arts of the Tribe, but I still had lessons from Ichiro in the ways of the clans. The warrior class was the complete opposite of the Tribe. They set great store by the admiration and respect of the world, and their reputation and standing in it. I had to learn their history and etiquette, courtesies, and language. I studied the archives of the Otori, going back for centuries, all the way to their half-mythical origins in the Emperor's family, until my head was reeling with names and genealogies.

The days shortened, the nights grew colder. The first frosts rimed the garden. Soon the snow would shut off the mountain passes, winter storms would close the port, and Hagi would be isolated until spring. The house had a different song now, muffled, soft, and sleeping.

Something had unlocked a mad hunger in me for learning. Kenji said it was the character of the Tribe surfacing after years of neglect. It embraced everything, from the most complex characters in writing to the demands of swordplay.

These I learned wholeheartedly, but I had a more divided response to Kenji's lessons. I did not find them difficult—they came all too naturally to me—but there was something about them that repelled me, something within me that resisted becoming what he wanted me to be.

"It's a game," he told me many times. "Play it like a game." But it was a game whose end was death. Kenji had been right in his reading of my character. I had been brought up to abhor murder, and I had a deep reluctance to take life.

He studied that aspect of me. It made him uneasy. He and Lord Shigeru often talked about ways to make me tougher.

"He has all the talents, save that one," Kenji said one evening in frustration. "And that lack makes all his talents a danger to him."

"You never know," Shigeru replied. "When the situation arises, it is amazing how the sword leaps in the hand, almost as though it has a will of its own."

"You were born that way, Shigeru, and all your training has reinforced it. My belief is that Takeo will hesitate in that moment."

"Unnh," the lord grunted, moving closer to the brazier

and pulling his coat around him. Snow had been falling all day. It lay piled in the garden, each tree coated, each lantern wearing a thick white cap. The sky had cleared and frost made the snow sparkle. Our breath hung in the air as we spoke.

Nobody else was awake, just the three of us, huddled round the brazier, warming our hands on cups of hot wine. It made me bold enough to ask, "Lord Otori must have killed many men?"

"I don't know that I've kept a count," he replied. "But apart from Yaegahara, probably not so very many. I have never killed an unarmed man, or killed for pleasure, as some are corrupted into. Better you should stay the way you are than come to that."

I wanted to ask, *Would you use an assassin to get revenge?* But I did not dare. It was true that I disliked cruelty and shrank from the idea of killing. But every day I learned more about Shigeru's desire for revenge. It seemed to seep from him into me, where it fed my own desire. That night I slid open the screens in the early hours of the morning and looked out over the garden. The waning moon and a single star lay close together in the sky, so low that they looked as if they were eavesdropping on the sleeping town. The air was knife-cold.

I could kill, I thought. *I could kill Iida.* And then: *I will kill him. I will learn how.*

A few days after that, I surprised Kenji and myself. His ability to be in two places at once still fooled me. I'd see the old man in his faded robe, sitting, watching me while I practiced some sleight of hand or backwards tumble, and then his voice would call me from outside the building. But this time, I felt or heard his breath, jumped towards him, caught him round the neck, and had him on the ground before I even thought, *Where is he?*

And to my amazement my hands went of their own accord to the spot on the artery in the neck where pressure brings death.

I had him there for only a moment. I let go and we stared at each other.

"Well," he said. "That's more like it!"

I looked at my long-fingered, clever hands as if they belonged to a stranger.

My hands did other things I had not known they could do. When I was practicing writing with Ichiro, my right hand would suddenly sketch a few strokes, and there would be one of my mountain birds about to fly off the paper, or the face of someone I did not know I remembered. Ichiro cuffed me round the head for it, but the drawings pleased him, and he showed them to Lord Shigeru.

He was delighted, and so was Kenji.

"It's a Kikuta trait," Kenji boasted, as proud as if he'd invented it himself. "Very useful. It gives Takeo a role to play, a perfect disguise. He's an artist: He can sketch in all sorts of places and no one will wonder what he can hear."

Lord Shigeru was equally practical. "Draw the one-armed man," he commanded.

The wolfish face seemed to jump of its own accord from the brush. Lord Shigeru stared at it. "I'll know him again," he muttered.

A drawing master was arranged, and through the winter days my new character evolved. By the time the snow melted, Tomasu, the half-wild boy who roamed the mountain and read only its animals and plants, was gone forever. I had become Takeo, quiet, outwardly gentle, an artist, somewhat bookish, a disguise that hid the ears and eyes that missed nothing, and the heart that was learning the lessons of revenge.

I did not know if this Takeo was real or just a construction created to serve the purposes of the Tribe, and the Otori.

· 4 ·

The bamboo grass had turned white-edged and the maples had put on their brocade robes. Junko brought Kaede old garments from Lady Noguchi, carefully unpicking them and resewing them with the faded parts turned inwards. As the days grew colder she was thankful that she was no longer in the castle, running through the courtyards and up and down steps as snow fell on frozen snow. Her work became more leisurely: She spent her days with the Noguchi women, engaged in sewing and household crafts, listening to stories and making up poems, learning to write in women's script. But she was far from happy.

Lady Noguchi found fault with everything about her:

She was repelled by her left-handedness, she compared her looks unfavorably to her daughters', she deplored her height and her thinness. She declared herself shocked by Kaede's lack of education in almost everything, never admitting that this might be her fault.

In private, Junko praised Kaede's pale skin, delicate limbs, and thick hair, and Kaede, gazing in the mirror whenever she could, thought that maybe she was beautiful. She knew men looked at her with desire, even here in the lord's residence, but she feared all men. Since the guard's assault on her, their nearness made her skin crawl. She dreaded the idea of marriage. Whenever a guest came to the house, she was afraid he might be her future husband. If she had to come into his presence with tea or wine, her heart raced and her hands shook, until Lady Noguchi decided she was too clumsy to wait on guests and must be confined to the women's quarters.

She grew bored and anxious. She quarreled with Lady Noguchi's daughters, scolded the maids over trifles, and was even irritable with Junko.

"The girl must be married," Lady Noguchi declared, and

to Kaede's horror a marriage was swiftly arranged with one of Lord Noguchi's retainers. Betrothal gifts were exchanged, and she recognized the man from her audience with the lord. Not only was he old—three times her age, married twice before, and physically repulsive to her—but she knew her own worth. The marriage was an insult to her and her family. She was being thrown away. She wept for nights and could not eat.

A week before the wedding, messengers came in the night, rousing the residence. Lady Noguchi summoned Kaede in rage.

"You are very unlucky, Lady Shirakawa. I think you must be cursed. Your betrothed husband is dead."

The man, celebrating the coming end to his widowhood, had been drinking with friends, had had a sudden seizure, and had fallen stone dead into the wine cups.

Kaede was sick with relief, but the second mortality was also held to be her fault. Two men had now died on her account, and the rumor began to spread that whoever desired her courted death.

She hoped it might put everyone off marrying her, but one evening, when the third month was drawing to a close and the trees were putting out bright new leaves, Junko whispered to her, "One of the Otori clan has been offered as my lady's husband."

They were embroidering, and Kaede lost the swaying rhythm of the stitching and jabbed herself with the needle, so hard that she drew blood. Junko quickly pulled the silk away before she stained it.

"Who is he?" she asked, putting her finger to her mouth and tasting the salt of her own blood.

"I don't know exactly. But Lord Iida himself is in favor, and the Tohan keen to seal the alliance with the Otori. Then they will control the whole of the Middle Country."

"How old is he?" Kaede forced herself to ask next.

"It's not clear yet, lady. But age does not matter in a husband."

Kaede took up the embroidery again: white cranes and blue turtles on a deep pink background—a wedding robe. "I wish it would never be finished!"

"Be happy, Lady Kaede. You will be leaving here. The Otori live in Hagi, by the sea. It's an honorable match for you."

"Marriage frightens me," Kaede said.

"Everyone's frightened of what they don't know! But women come to enjoy it; you'll see." Junko chuckled to herself.

Kaede remembered the hands of the guard, his strength, his desire, and felt revulsion rise in her. Her own hands, usually deft and quick, slowed. Junko scolded her, but not unkindly, and for the rest of the day treated her with great gentleness.

A few days later she was summoned to Lord Noguchi. She had heard the tramp of horses' feet and the shouts of strange men as guests arrived, but had as usual kept out of the way. It was with trepidation that she entered the audience room, but to her surprise and joy, her father was seated in a place of honor, at Lord Noguchi's side.

As she bowed to the ground she saw the delight leap into his face. She was proud that he saw her in a more honorable position now. She vowed she would never do anything to bring him sorrow or dishonor.

When she was told to sit up, she tried to take a discreet look at him. His hair was thinner and grayer, his face more lined. She longed for news of her mother and sisters; she hoped she would be granted some time alone with him.

"Lady Shirakawa," Lord Noguchi began. "We have received an offer for you in marriage, and your father has come to give his consent."

Kaede bowed low again, murmuring, "Lord Noguchi."

"It is a great honor for you. It will seal the alliance between the Tohan and the Otori, and unite three ancient families. Lord Iida himself will attend your wedding: Indeed, he wants it to take place in Inuyama. Since your mother is not well, a relative of your family, Lady Maruyama, is going to escort you to Tsuwano. Your husband is to be Otori Shigeru, a nephew of the Otori lords. He and his retainers will meet you in Tsuwano. I don't think any other arrangements need to be made. It's all very satisfactory."

Kaede's eyes had flown to her father's face when she heard her mother was not well. She hardly took in Lord Noguchi's subsequent words. Later she realized that the whole affair had been arranged with the least possible inconvenience and expense to himself: some robes for travel and to be married in, possibly a maid to accompany her. Truly he had come out of the whole exchange well.

He was joking now about the dead guard. The color rose in Kaede's face. Her father's eyes were cast down.

I'm glad he lost a man over me, she thought savagely. *May he lose a hundred more.*

Her father was to return home the following day, his wife's illness preventing a longer stay. In his expansive mood, Lord Noguchi urged him to spend time with his daughter. Kaede led her father to the small room overlooking the garden. The air was warm, heavy with the scents of spring. A bush warbler called from the pine tree. Junko served them tea. Her courtesy and attentiveness lightened her father's mood.

"I am glad you have one friend here, Kaede," he murmured.

"What is the news of my mother?" she said, anxiously.

"I wish it were better. I fear the rainy season will weaken her further. But this marriage has lifted her spirits. The Otori are a great family, and Lord Shigeru, it seems, a fine man. His reputation is good. He is well liked and respected. It's all we could have hoped for you—more than we could have hoped."

"Then I am happy with it," she said, lying to please him.

He gazed out at the cherry blossoms, each tree heavy, dreaming in its own beauty. "Kaede, the matter of the dead guard . . ."

"It was not my fault," she said hastily. "Captain Arai acted to protect me. All the fault was with the dead man."

He sighed. "They are saying that you are dangerous to men—that Lord Otori should beware. Nothing must happen to prevent this wedding. Do you understand me, Kaede? If it does not go ahead—if the fault can be laid on you—we are all as good as dead."

Kaede bowed, her heart heavy. Her father was like a stranger to her.

"It's been a burden on you to carry the safety of our family for all these years. Your mother and your sisters miss you. I myself would have had things differently, if I could choose over again. Maybe if I had taken part in the battle of Yaegahara, had not waited to see who would emerge the victor but had joined Iida from the start . . . but it's all past now, and cannot be brought back. In his way Lord Noguchi has kept his side of the bargain. You are alive; you are to make a good marriage. I know you will not fail us now."

"Father," she said as a small breeze blew suddenly through the garden, and the pink and white petals drifted like snow to the ground.

The next day her father left. Kaede watched him ride

away with his retainers. They had been with her family since before her own birth, and she remembered some of them by name: her father's closest friend, Shoji, and young Amano, who was only a few years older than she was. After they had left through the castle gate, the horses' hooves crushing the cherry blossoms that carpeted the shallow cobbled steps, she ran to the bailey to watch them disappear along the banks of the river. Finally the dust settled, the town dogs quieted, and they were gone.

The next time she saw her father she would be a married woman, making the formal return to her parents' home.

Kaede went back to the residence, scowling to keep her tears at bay. Her spirits were not improved by hearing a stranger's voice. Someone was chatting away to Junko. It was the sort of chat that she most despised, in a little-girl voice with a high-pitched giggle. She could just imagine the girl, tiny, with round cheeks like a doll, a small-stepped walk like a bird's, and a head that was always bobbing and bowing.

When she hurried into the room, Junko and the strange girl were working on her clothes, making the last adjustments, folding and stitching. The Noguchi were losing no time in getting rid of her. Bamboo baskets and paulownia wood boxes stood ready to be packed. The sight of them upset Kaede further.

"What is this person doing here?" she demanded irritably.

The girl flattened herself to the floor, overdoing it, as Kaede had known she would.

"This is Shizuka," Junko said. "She is to travel with Lady Kaede to Inuyama."

"I don't want her," Kaede replied. "I want you to come with me."

"Lady, it's not possible for me to leave. Lady Noguchi would never permit it."

"Then tell her to send someone else."

Shizuka, still facedown on the ground, gave what sounded like a sob. Kaede, sure that it was feigned, was unmoved.

"You are upset, lady. The news of the marriage, your father's departure . . ." Junko tried to placate her. "She's a good girl, very pretty, very clever. Sit up, Shizuka: Let Lady Shirakawa look at you."

The girl raised herself but did not look directly at Kaede. From her downcast eyes, tears trickled. She sniffed once or twice. "Lady, please don't send me away. I'll do anything for you. I swear, you'll never have anyone look after you better than me. I'll carry you in the rain, I'll let you warm your feet on me in the cold." Her tears seemed to have dried and she was smiling again.

"You didn't warn me how beautiful Lady Shirakawa is," she said to Junko. "No wonder men die for her!"

"Don't say that!" Kaede cried. She walked angrily to the doorway. Two gardeners were cleaning leaves off the moss, one by one. "I'm tired of having it said of me."

"It will always be said," Junko remarked. "It is part of the lady's life now."

"I wish men would die for me." Shizuka laughed. "But they just seem to fall in and out of love with me as easily as I do with them!"

Kaede did not turn around. The girl shuffled on her knees to the boxes and began folding the garments again, singing softly as she did it. Her voice was clear and true. It was an old ballad about the little village in the pine forest, the girl, the young man. Kaede thought she recalled it from her childhood. It brought clearly into her mind the fact that her childhood was over, that she was to marry a stranger, that she would never know love. Maybe people in villages could fall in love, but for someone in her position it was not even to be considered.

She strode across the room and, kneeling next to Shizuka, took the garment roughly from her. "If you're going to do it, do it properly!"

"Yes, lady." Shizuka flattened herself again, crushing the robes around her. "Thank you, lady, you'll never regret it!"

As she sat up again she murmured, "People say Lord Arai takes a great interest in Lady Shirakawa. They talk of his regard for her honor."

"Do you know Arai?" Kaede said sharply.

"I am from his town, lady. From Kumamoto."

Junko was smiling broadly. "I can say good-bye with a calm mind if I know you have Shizuka to look after you."

So Shizuka became part of Kaede's life, irritating and amusing her in equal measures. She loved gossip, spread rumors without the least concern, was always disappearing into the kitchens, the stables, the castle, and coming back bursting with stories. She was popular with everyone and had no fear of men. As far as Kaede could see, they were more afraid of her, in awe of her teasing words and sharp tongue. On the surface she appeared slapdash, but her care of Kaede was meticulous. She massaged away her headaches, brought ointments made of herbs and beeswax to soften her creamy skin, plucked her eyebrows into a more gentle shape. Kaede came to rely on her, and eventually to trust her. Despite herself, Shizuka made her laugh, and she brought her for the first time into contact with the outside world, from which Kaede had been isolated.

So Kaede learned of the uneasy relationships between the clans, the many bitter grudges left after Yaegahara, the alliances Iida was trying to form with the Otori and the Seishuu, the constant to-and-fro of men vying for position and preparing once again for war. She also learned of the Hidden, Iida's persecution of them, and his demands that his allies should do the same.

She had never heard of such people and thought at first that Shizuka was making them up. Then one evening Shizuka, uncharacteristically subdued, whispered to her that men and women had been found in a small village and brought to Noguchi in basket cages. They were to be hung from the castle walls until they died of hunger and thirst. The crows pecked at them while they were still alive.

"Why? What crime did they commit?" she questioned.

"They say there is a secret god, who sees everything and who they cannot offend or deny. They would rather die."

Kaede shivered. "Why does Lord Iida hate them so?"

Shizuka glanced over her shoulder, even though they were alone in the room. "They say the secret god will punish Iida in the afterlife."

"But Iida is the most powerful lord in the Three Countries. He can do what he wants. They have no right to judge him." The idea that a lord's actions should be judged by ordinary village people was ludicrous to Kaede.

"The Hidden believe that their god sees everyone as equal. There are no lords in their god's eyes. Only those who believe in him and those who do not."

Kaede frowned. No wonder Iida wanted to stamp them out. She would have asked more but Shizuka changed the subject.

"Lady Maruyama is expected any day now. Then we will begin our journey."

"It will be good to leave this place of death," Kaede said.

"Death is everywhere." Shizuka took the comb and with long, even strokes ran it through Kaede's hair. "Lady

Maruyama is a close relative of yours. Did you meet her when you were a child?"

"If I did I don't remember it. She is my mother's cousin, I believe, but I know very little about her. Have you met her?"

"I have seen her," Shizuka said with a laugh. "People like me don't really meet people like her!"

"Tell me about her," Kaede said.

"As you know, she owns a large domain in the southwest. Her husband and her son are both dead, and her daughter, who would inherit, is a hostage in Inuyama. It is well known that the lady is no friend to the Tohan, despite her husband being of that clan. Her stepdaughter is married to Iida's cousin. There were rumors that after her husband's death, his family had her son poisoned. First Iida offered his brother to her in marriage, but she refused him. Now they say he himself wants to marry her."

"Surely he is married already, and has a son," Kaede interrupted.

"None of Lady Iida's other children has survived beyond childhood, and her health is very poor. It might fail at any time."

In other words, he might murder her, Kaede thought, but did not dare say it.

"Anyway," Shizuka went on, "Lady Maruyama will never marry him, so they say, and she will not allow her daughter to either."

"She makes her own decisions about who she will marry? She sounds like a powerful woman."

"Maruyama is the last of the great domains to be inherited through the female line," Shizuka explained. "This gives her more power than other women. And then, she has other powers that seem almost magic. She bewitches people to get her own way."

"Do you believe such things?"

"How else can you explain her survival? Her late husband's family, Lord Iida, and most of the Tohan would crush her, but she survives, despite having lost her son to them and seeing them hold her daughter."

Kaede felt her heart twist in sympathy. "Why do women have to suffer this way? Why don't we have the freedom men have?"

"It's the way the world is," Shizuka replied. "Men are stronger and not held back by feelings of tenderness or mercy. Women fall in love with them, but they do not return that love."

"I will never fall in love," Kaede said.

"Better not to," Shizuka agreed, and laughed. She prepared the beds, and they lay down to sleep. Kaede thought for a long time about the lady who held power like a man, the lady who had lost a son and as good as lost a daughter. She thought of the girl, hostage in the Iida stronghold at Inuyama, and pitied her.

Lady Noguchi's reception room was decorated in the mainland style, the doors and screens painted with scenes of mountains and pine trees. Kaede disliked all the pictures, finding them heavy, their gold leaf flamboyant and ostentatious, save the one farthest to the left. This was of two pheasants, so lifelike that they looked as if they might suddenly take flight. Their eyes were bright, their heads cocked. They listened to the conversation in the room with more animation than most of the women who knelt before Lady Noguchi.

On the lady's right sat the visitor, Lady Maruyama. Lady Noguchi made a sign to Kaede to approach a little closer. She bent to the floor and listened to the two-tongued words being spoken above her head.

"Of course we are distraught at losing Lady Kaede: She has been like our own daughter. And we hesitate to burden Lady Maruyama. We ask only that Kaede be allowed to accompany you as far as Tsuwano. There the Otori lords will meet her."

"Lady Shirakawa is to be married into the Otori family?" Kaede liked the low, gentle voice she heard. She raised her head very slightly so she could see the lady's small hands folded in her lap.

"Yes, to Lord Otori Shigeru," Lady Noguchi purred. "It is a great honor. Of course, my husband is very close to Lord Iida, who himself desires the match."

Kaede saw the hands clench until the blood drained from them. After a pause, so long it was almost impolite, Lady Maruyama said, "Lord Otori Shigeru? Lady Shirakawa is fortunate indeed."

"The lady has met him? I have never had that pleasure."

"I know Lord Otori very slightly," Lady Maruyama replied. "Sit up, Lady Shirakawa, let me see your face."

Kaede raised her head.

"You are so young!" the older woman exclaimed.

"I am fifteen, lady."

"Only a little older than my daughter." Lady Maruyama's voice was thin and faint. Kaede dared look in the dark eyes, with their perfect shape. The pupils were dilated as if in shock, and the lady's face was whiter than any powder could have made it. Then she seemed to regain some control over herself. A smile came to her lips, though it did not reach her eyes.

What have I done to her? Kaede thought in confusion. She had felt instinctively drawn to her. She thought Shizuka was right: Lady Maruyama could get anyone to do anything for her. Her beauty was faded, it was true, but somehow the faint lines round the eyes and mouth simply added to the character and strength of the face. Now the coldness of her expression wounded Kaede deeply.

She doesn't like me, the girl thought, with an overwhelming sense of disappointment.

· 5 ·

The snow melted and the house and garden began to sing with water again. I had been in Hagi for six months. I had learned to read, write, and draw. I had learned to kill in many different ways, although I was yet to put any one of them into practice. I felt I could hear the intentions of men's hearts, and I'd learned other useful skills, though these were not so much taught to me by Kenji as drawn up out of me. I could be in two places at once, and take on invisibility, and could silence dogs with a look that dropped them immediately into sleep. This last trick I discovered on my own, and kept it from Kenji, for he taught me deviousness along with everything else.

I used these skills whenever I grew tired of the confines of the house, and its relentless routine of study, practice, and obedience to my two severe teachers. I found it all too easy to distract the guards, put the dogs to sleep, and slip through the gate without anyone seeing me. Even Ichiro and Kenji more than once were convinced I was sitting somewhere quietly in the house with ink and brush, when I was out with Fumio, exploring the back alleys around the port, swimming in the river, listening to the sailors and the fishermen, breathing in the heady mix of salt air, hemp ropes and nets, and seafood in all its forms, raw, steamed, grilled, made into little dumplings or hearty stews that made our stomachs growl with hunger. I caught the different accents, from the West, from the islands, even from the mainland, and listened to conversations no one knew could be overheard, learning always about the lives of the people, their fears and their desires.

Sometimes I went out on my own, crossing the river either by the fish weir or swimming. I explored the lands on the far side, going deep into the mountains where farmers had their secret fields, tucked away among the trees, unseen and therefore untaxed. I saw the new green leaves burgeon in the coppices, and heard the chestnut groves come alive with buzzing insects seeking the pollen on their golden catkins. I heard the farmers buzz like insects, too, grumbling endlessly about the Otori lords, the ever-increasing burden of taxes. And time and again Lord Shigeru's name came up, and I learned of the bitterness held by more than half the population that it was his uncles, and not he, in the castle. This was treason, spoken of only at night or deep in the forest, when no one could overhear except me, and I said nothing about it to anyone.

Spring burst on the landscape; the air was warm, the whole earth alive. I was filled with a restlessness I did not understand. I was looking for something, but had no idea what it was. Kenji took me to the pleasure district, and I slept with girls there, not telling him I had already visited the same places with Fumio, and finding only a brief release from my longing. The girls filled me with pity as much as lust. They reminded me of the girls I'd grown up with in Mino. They came in all likelihood from similar families, sold into prostitution by their starving parents. Some of them were barely out of childhood, and I searched their faces, looking for my sisters' features. Shame often crept over me, but I did not stay away.

The spring festivals came, packing the shrines and the streets with people. Drums shouted every night, the drummers' faces and arms glistening with sweat in the lantern light, possessed beyond exhaustion. I could not resist the fever of the celebrations, the frenzied ecstasy of the crowds. One night I'd been out with Fumio, following the god's statue as it was carried through the streets by a throng of struggling, excited men. I had just said good-bye to him, when I was shoved into someone, almost stepping on him. He turned towards me and I recognized him: It was the traveler who had stayed at our house and tried to warn us of Iida's persecution. A short squat man, with an ugly, shrewd face, he was a kind of peddler who sometimes came to Mino. Before I could turn away I saw the flash of recognition in his eyes, and saw pity spring there too.

He shouted to make himself heard above the yelling crowd. "Tomasu!"

I shook my head, making my face and eyes blank, but he was insistent. He tried to pull me out of the crowd into a passageway. "Tomasu, it's you, isn't it—the boy from Mino?"

"You're mistaken," I said. "I know no one called Tomasu."

"Everyone thought you were dead!"

"I don't know what you're talking about." I laughed, as if at a great joke, and tried to push my way back into the crowd. He grabbed my arm to detain me and as he opened his mouth I knew what he was going to say.

"Your mother's dead. They killed her. They killed them all. You're the only one left! How did you get away?" He tried to pull my face close to his. I could smell his breath, his sweat.

"You're drunk, old man!" I said. "My mother is alive and well in Hofu, last I heard." I pushed him off and reached for my knife. "I am of the Otori clan." I let anger replace my laughter.

He backed away. "Forgive me, lord. It was a mistake. I see now you are not who I thought you were." He was a little drunk, but fear was fast sobering him.

Through my mind flashed several thoughts at once, the most pressing being that now I would have to kill this man, this harmless peddler who had tried to warn my family. I saw exactly how it would be done: I would lead him deeper into the passageway, take him off balance, slip the knife into the artery in the neck, slash upwards, then let him fall, lie like a drunk, and bleed to death. Even if anyone saw me, no one would dare apprehend me.

The crowd surged past us; the knife was in my hand. He

dropped to the ground, his head in the dirt, pleading incoherently for his life.

I cannot kill him, I thought, and then: *There is no need to kill him. He's decided I'm not Tomasu, and even if he has his doubts, he will never dare voice them to anyone. He is one of the Hidden, after all.*

I backed away and let the crowd carry me as far as the gates of the shrine. Then I slipped through the throng to the path that ran along the bank of the river. Here it was dark, deserted, but I could still hear the shouts of the excited crowd, the chants of the priests, and the dull tolling of the temple bell. The river lapped and sucked at the boats, the docks, the reeds. I remembered the first night I spent in Lord Shigeru's house. *The river is always at the door. The world is always outside. And it is in the world that we must live.*

The dogs, sleepy and docile, followed me with their eyes as I went through the gate, but the guards did not notice. Sometimes on these occasions I would creep into the guardroom and take them by surprise, but this night I had no stomach for jokes. I thought bitterly how slow and unobservant they were, how easy it would be for another member of the Tribe to enter, as the assassin had done. Then I was filled with revulsion for this world of stealth, duplicity, and intrigue that I was so skilled in. I longed to be Tomasu again, running down the mountain to my mother's house.

The corners of my eyes were burning. The garden was full of the scents and sounds of spring. In the moonlight the early blossoms gleamed with a fragile whiteness. Their purity pierced my heart. How was it possible for the world to be so beautiful and so cruel at the same time?

Lamps on the veranda flickered and guttered in the warm breeze. Kenji was sitting in the shadows. He called to me, "Lord Shigeru has been scolding Ichiro for losing you. I told him, 'You can gentle a fox but you'll never turn it into a house dog!'" He saw my face as I came into the light. "What happened?"

"My mother is dead." *Only children cry. Men and women endure.* Within my heart the child Tomasu was crying, but Takeo was dry-eyed.

Kenji drew me closer and whispered, "Who told you?"

"Someone I knew from Mino was at the shrine."

"He recognized you?"

"He thought he did. I persuaded him he was wrong. But while he still thought I was Tomasu, he told me of my mother's death."

"I'm sorry for it," Kenji said perfunctorily. "You killed him, I hope."

I didn't reply. I didn't need to. He knew almost as soon as he'd formed the question. He thwacked me on the back in exasperation, as Ichiro did when I missed a stroke in a character. "You're a fool, Takeo!"

"He was unarmed, harmless. He knew my family."

"It's just as I feared. You let pity stay your hand. Don't you know the man whose life you spare will always hate you? All you did was convince him you are Tomasu."

"Why should he die because of my destiny? What benefit would his death bring? None!"

"It's the disasters his life, his living tongue, may bring that concern me," Kenji replied, and went inside to tell Lord Shigeru.

I was in disgrace in the household and forbidden to wander alone in the town. Kenji kept a closer eye on me, and I found it almost impossible to evade him. It didn't keep me from trying. As always, an obstacle only had to be set before me for me to seek to overcome it. I infuriated him by my lack of obedience, but my skills grew even more acute, and I came to have more and more confidence in them.

Lord Shigeru spoke to me of my mother's death after Kenji had told him of my failure as an assassin. "You wept for her the first night we met. There must be no sign of grief now. You don't know who is watching you."

So the grief remained unexpressed, in my heart. At night I silently repeated the prayers of the Hidden for my mother's soul, and for my sisters'. But I did not say the prayers of forgiveness she had taught me. I had no intention of loving my enemies. I let my grief feed my desire for revenge.

That night was also the last time I saw Fumio. When I managed to evade Kenji and get to the port again, the Terada ships had vanished. I learned from the other fishermen that they had left one night, finally driven into exile by high taxes and unfair regulations. The rumors were that they had fled to Oshima, where the family originally hailed from. With that remote island as a base, they would almost certainly turn to piracy.

Around this time, before the plum rains began, Lord Shigeru became very interested in construction and proceeded with his plans to build a tea room on one end of the house.

I went with him to choose the wood, the cedar trunks that would support floor and roof, the slabs of cypress for the walls. The smell of sawn wood reminded me of the mountains, and the carpenters had the characteristics of the men of my village, being mostly taciturn but given to sudden outbursts of laughter over their unfathomable jokes. I found myself slipping back into my old patterns of speech, using words from the village I had not used for months. Sometimes my slang even made them chuckle.

Lord Shigeru was intrigued by all the stages of building, from seeing the trees felled in the forest to the preparation of the planks and the different methods of laying floors. We made many visits to the lumberyard, accompanied by the master carpenter, Shiro, a man who seemed to be fashioned from the same material as the wood he loved so much, brother to the cedar and the cypress. He spoke of the character and spirit of each type of wood, and what it brings from the forest into the house.

"Each wood has its own sound," he said. "Every house has its own song."

I had thought only I knew how a house can sing. I'd been listening to Lord Shigeru's house for months now, had heard its song quiet into winter music, had listened to its beams and walls as it pressed closer to the ground under the weight of snow, froze and thawed and shrank and stretched. Now it sang again of water.

Shiro was watching me as though he knew my thoughts.

"I've heard Lord Iida has ordered a floor to be made that sings like a nightingale," he said. "But who needs to make a floor sing like a bird when it already has its own song?"

"What's the purpose of such a floor?" Lord Shigeru asked, seemingly idly.

"He's afraid of assassination. It's one more piece of protection. No one can cross the floor without it starting to chirp."

"How is it made?"

The old man took a piece of half-made flooring and explained how the joists were placed so the boards squeaked. "They have them, I'm told, in the capital. Most people want a silent floor. They'd reject a noisy one, make you lay it again. But Iida can't sleep at night. He's afraid someone will creep in on him—and now he lies awake, afraid his floor will sing!" He chuckled to himself.

"Could you make such a floor?" Lord Shigeru inquired.

Shiro grinned at me. "I can make a floor so quiet, even Takeo can't hear it. I reckon I can make one that would sing."

"Takeo will help you," the lord announced. "He needs to know exactly how it is constructed."

I did not dare ask why then. I already had a fair idea, but I did not want to put it into words. The discussion moved on to the tea room, and while Shiro directed its building, he made a small singing floor, a boardwalk that replaced the verandas of the house, and I watched every board laid, every joist and every peg.

Chiyo complained that the squeaking gave her a headache, and that it sounded more like mice than any bird. But eventually the household grew used to it, and the noises became part of the everyday song of the house.

The floor amused Kenji to no end: He thought it would keep me inside. Lord Shigeru said no more about why I had to know how the floor was made, but I imagine he knew the pull it would have on me. I listened to it all day long. I knew exactly who was walking on it by their tread. I could predict the next note of the floor's song. I tried to walk on it without awakening the birds. It was hard—Shiro had done his job well—but not impossible. I had watched the floor being made. I knew there was nothing enchanted about it. It was just a matter of time before I mastered it. With the almost fanatical patience that I knew now was a trait of the Tribe, I practiced crossing the floor.

The rains began. One night the air was so hot and humid, I could not sleep. I went to get a drink from the cistern and then stood in the doorway, looking at the floor stretching away from me. I knew I was going to cross it without waking anyone.

I moved swiftly, my feet knowing where to step and with how much pressure. The birds remained silent. I felt the deep pleasure, no kin to elation, that acquiring the skills of the Tribe brings, until I heard the sound of breathing, and turned to see Lord Shigeru watching me.

"You heard me," I said, disappointed.

"No, I was already awake. Can you do it again?"

I stayed crouched where I was for a moment, retreating into myself in the way of the Tribe, letting everything drain from me except my awareness of the noises of the night. Then I ran back across the nightingale floor. The birds slept on.

I thought about Iida lying awake in Inuyama, listening for the singing birds. I imagined myself creeping across the floor towards him, completely silent, completely undetected.

If Lord Shigeru was thinking the same thing, he did not mention it. All he said now was, "I'm disappointed in Shiro. I thought his floor would outwit you."

Neither of us said, *But will Iida's?* Nevertheless the question lay between us, in the heavy night air of the sixth month.

The teahouse was also finished, and we often shared tea there in the evenings, reminding me of the first time I had tasted the expensive green brew prepared by Lady Maruyama. I felt Lord Shigeru had built it with her in mind, but he never mentioned it. At the door of the tea room grew a twin-trunked camellia; maybe it was this symbol of married love that started everyone talking about the desirability of marriage. Ichiro in particular urged the lord to set about finding another wife. "Your mother's death, and Takeshi's, have been an excuse for some time. But you have been unmarried for nearly ten years now, and have no children. It's unheard of!"

The servants gossiped about it, forgetting that I could hear them clearly from every part of the house. The general opinion among them was in fact close to the truth, although they did not really believe it themselves. They decided Lord Shigeru must be in love with some unsuitable or unobtainable woman. They must have sworn fidelity to each other, the girls sighed, since to their regret he had never invited any of them to share his bed. The older women, more realistic, pointed out that these things might occur in songs but had no bearing on the everyday life of the warrior class. "Maybe he prefers boys," Haruka, the boldest of the girls, replied, adding in a fit of giggles. "Ask Takeo!" Whereupon Chiyo said preferring boys was one thing, and marriage was another. The two had nothing to do with each other.

Lord Shigeru evaded all these questions of marriage, saying he was more concerned with the process of my adoption. For months nothing had been heard from the clan, except that the subject was still under deliberation. The Otori had more pressing concerns to attend to. Iida had started his summer campaign in the East, and fief after fief had either joined the Tohan or been conquered and annihilated. Soon he would turn his attention again to the Middle Country. The Otori had grown used to peace. Lord Shigeru's uncles were disinclined to confront Iida and plunge the fief into war again. Yet, the idea of submitting to the Tohan rankled with most of the clan.

Hagi was rife with rumors, and tense. Kenji was uneasy. He watched me all the time, and the constant supervision made me irritable.

"There are more Tohan spies in town every week," he said. "Sooner or later one of them is going to recognize Takeo. Let me take him away."

"Once he is legally adopted and under the protection of the clan, Iida will think twice about touching him," Lord Shigeru replied.

"I think you underestimate him. He will dare anything."

"Maybe in the East. But not in the Middle Country."

They often argued about it, Kenji pressing the lord to let me go away with him, Lord Shigeru evading him, refusing to take the danger seriously, holding that once I was adopted I would be safer in Hagi than anywhere.

I caught Kenji's mood. I was on guard all the time, always alert, always watching. The only time I found peace was when I was absorbed in learning new skills. I became obsessive about honing my talents.

Finally the message came at the end of the seventh

month: Lord Shigeru was to bring me to the castle the next day, where his uncles would receive me and a decision would be given.

Chiyo scrubbed me, washed and trimmed my hair, and brought out clothes that were new but subdued in color. Ichiro went over and over all the etiquette and the courtesies, the language I should use, how low I should bow. "Don't let us down," he hissed at me as we left. "After all he has done for you, don't let Lord Shigeru down."

Kenji did not come with us but said he would follow us as far as the castle gate. "Just keep your ears open," he told me—as if it were possible for me to do anything else.

I was on Raku, the pale gray horse with the black mane and tail. Lord Shigeru rode ahead of me on his black horse, Kyu, with five or six retainers. As we approached the castle I was seized by panic. Its power as it loomed ahead of us, its complete dominance over the town unnerved me. What was I doing, pretending to be a lord, a warrior? The Otori lords would take one look at me and see me for what I was: the son of a peasant woman and an assassin. Worse, I felt horribly exposed, riding through the crowded street. I imagined that everyone was looking at me.

Raku felt the panic and tensed. A sudden movement in the crowd made him shy slightly. Without thinking, I let my breathing slow and softened my body. He quieted immediately. But his action had spun us around, and as I turned his head back I caught sight of a man in the street. I only saw his face for a moment, but I knew him at once. I saw the empty sleeve on his right-hand side. I had drawn his likeness for Lord Shigeru and Kenji. It was the man who had pursued me up the mountain path, whose right arm Jato had sliced through.

He did not appear to be watching me, and I had no way of knowing if he had recognized me. I drew the horse back and rode on. I don't believe I gave the slightest sign I had noticed him. The entire episode lasted no more than a minute.

Strangely, it calmed me. *This is real*, I thought. *Not a game. Maybe I am pretending to be something I'm not, but if I fail in it, it means death.* And then I thought, *I am Kikuta. I am of the Tribe. I am a match for anyone.*

As we crossed the moat I spotted Kenji in the crowd, an old man in a faded robe. Then the main gates were opened to us, and we rode through into the first courtyard.

Here we dismounted. The men stayed with the horses, and Lord Shigeru and I were met by an elderly man, the steward, who took us to the residence.

It was an imposing and gracious building on the seaward side of the castle, protected by a smaller bailey. A moat surrounded it all the way to the seawall, and inside the moat was a large, beautifully designed garden. A small, densely wooded hill rose behind the castle; above the trees rose the curved roof of a shrine.

The sun had come out briefly, and the stones steamed in the heat. I could feel the sweat forming on my forehead and in my armpits. I could hear the sea hissing at the rocks below the wall. I wished I were swimming in it.

We took off our sandals, and maids came with cool water to wash our feet. The steward led us into the house. It seemed to go on forever, room after room stretching away, each one lavishly and expensively decorated. Finally we came to an antechamber where he asked us to wait for a little while. We sat on the floor for what seemed like an hour at least. At first I was outraged—at the insult to Lord Shigeru, at the extravagant luxury of the house, which I knew came from the taxes imposed on the farmers. I wanted to tell Lord Shigeru about my sighting of Iida's man in Hagi, but I did not dare speak. He seemed engrossed in the painting on the doors: a gray heron stood in a teal-green river, gazing at a pink and gold mountain.

Finally I remembered Kenji's advice and spent the rest of the time listening to the house. It did not sing of the river, like Lord Shigeru's, but had a deeper and graver note, underpinned by the constant surge of the sea. I counted how many different footsteps I could hear, and decided there were fifty-three people in the household. I could hear three children in the garden, playing with two puppies. I heard the ladies talking about a boat trip they were hoping to make if the weather held.

Then from deep inside the house I heard two men talking quietly. I heard Shigeru's name mentioned. I realized I was listening to his uncles uttering things they would let no one but each other hear.

"The main thing is to get Shigeru to agree to the marriage," said one. His was the older voice, I thought, stronger and more opinionated. I frowned, wondering what he meant. Hadn't we come to discuss adoption?

"He's always resisted marrying again," said the other, slightly deferential, presumably younger. "And to marry to seal the Tohan alliance, when he has always opposed it . . . It may simply bring him out in the open."

"We are at a very dangerous time," the older man said. "News came yesterday about the situation in the West. It seems the Seishuu are preparing to challenge Iida. Arai, the lord of Kumamoto, considers himself offended by the Noguchi, and is raising an army to fight them and the Tohan before winter."

"Is Shigeru in contact with him? It could give him the opportunity he needs. . . ."

"You don't need to spell it out," his brother replied. "I'm only too aware of Shigeru's popularity with the clan. If he is in alliance with Arai, together they could take on Iida."

"Unless we . . . shall we say, disarm him."

"The marriage would answer very well. It would take Shigeru to Inuyama, where he'll be under Iida's eye for a while. And the lady in question, Shirakawa Kaede, has a certain very useful reputation."

"You're not suggesting . . . ?"

"Two men have already died in connection with her. It would be regrettable if Shigeru were the third, but hardly our fault."

The younger man laughed quietly in a way that made me want to kill him. I breathed deeply, trying to calm my fury.

"What if he continues to refuse to marry?" he asked.

"We make it a condition of this adoption whim of his. I can't see how it will do us any harm."

"I've been trying to trace the boy," the younger man said, his voice taking on the pedantic tone of an archivist. "I don't see how he can be related to Shigeru's late mother. There is no sign of him in the genealogies."

"I suppose he is illegitimate," the older man said. "I've heard he looks like Takeshi."

"Yes, his looks make it hard to argue against any Otori blood, but if we were to adopt all our illegitimate children . . ."

"Ordinarily of course it would be out of the question. But just now . . ."

"I agree."

I heard the floor creak slightly as they stood.

"One last thing," the older brother said. "You assured me Shintaro would not fail. What went wrong?"

"I've been trying to find out. Apparently this boy heard him and woke Shigeru. Shintaro took poison."

"He heard him? Is he also from the Tribe?"

"It's possible. A Muto Kenji turned up at Shigeru's last year: Some kind of tutor is the official story, but I don't think he is giving the usual kind of instruction." Again the younger brother laughed, making my flesh crawl. But I also felt a deep scorn for them. They had been told of my acute hearing, yet they did not imagine it could apply to them, here in their own house.

The slight tremor of their footsteps moved from the inner room, where this secret conversation had been taking place, into the room behind the painted doors.

A few moments later the elderly man came back, slid the doors open gently, and indicated that we should enter the audience chamber. The two lords sat side by side on low chairs. Several men knelt along each side of the room. Lord Shigeru immediately bowed to the ground, and I did the same, but not before I had taken a quick look at these two brothers, against whom my heart was already bitter in the extreme.

The older one, Lord Otori Shoichi, was tall but not particularly muscular. His face was lean and gaunt; he wore a small mustache and beard, and his hair was already going gray. The younger one, Masahiro, was shorter and squatter.

He held himself very erect, as small men do. He had no beard; his face was sallow in color, and spotted with several large black moles. His hair was still black, but thin. In both of them, the distinctive Otori features, the prominent cheek-bones and curved nose, were marred by the defects of character that made them both cruel and weak.

"Lord Shigeru—nephew—you are very welcome," Shoichi said graciously.

Lord Shigeru sat up, but I remained with my forehead on the floor.

"You have been much in our thoughts," Masahiro said. "We have been very concerned for you. Your brother's passing away, coming so soon after your mother's death and your own illness, has been a heavy burden to you."

The words sounded kindly, but I knew they were spoken by the second tongue.

"I thank you for your concern," Shigeru replied, "but you must allow me to correct you in one thing. My brother did not pass away. He was murdered."

He said it without emotion, as if simply stating a fact. No one in the room made any reaction. A deep silence followed.

Lord Shoichi broke it by saying, with feigned cheerfulness, "And this is your young charge? He is also welcome. What is his name?"

"We call him Takeo," Shigeru replied.

"Apparently he has very sharp hearing?" Masahiro leaned forward a little.

"Nothing out of the ordinary," Shigeru said. "We all have sharp hearing when we are young."

"Sit up, young man," Masahiro said to me. When I did so, he studied my face for a few moments and then asked, "Who is in the garden?"

I furrowed my brow as if the idea of counting them had only just occurred to me. "Two children and a dog," I hazarded. "A gardener by the wall?"

"And how many people in the household would you estimate?"

I shrugged slightly, then thought it was very impolite and tried to turn it into a bow. "Upwards of forty-five? Forgive me, Lord Otori, I have no great talents."

"How many are there, brother?" Lord Shoichi asked.

"Fifty-three, I believe."

"Impressive," the older brother said, but I heard his sigh of relief.

I bowed to the floor again and, feeling safer there, stayed low.

"We have delayed in this matter of adoption for so long, Shigeru, because of our uncertainty as to your state of mind. Grief seemed to have made you very unstable."

"There is no uncertainty in my mind," Shigeru replied. "I have no living children, and now that Takeshi is dead, I have no heir. I have obligations to this boy, and he to me, that must be fulfilled. He is already accepted by my household and has made his home with us. I ask that this situation be formalized and that he be adopted into the Otori clan."

"What does the boy say?"

"Speak, Takeo," Lord Shigeru prompted me.

I sat up, swallowing hard, suddenly overwhelmed by a deep emotion. I thought of the horse, shying as my heart shied now. "I owe my life to Lord Otori. He owes me nothing. The honor he is bestowing is far too great for me, but if it is his—and your lordships'—will, I accept with all my heart. I will serve the Otori clan faithfully all my life."

"Then it may be so," Lord Shoichi said.

"The documents are prepared," Lord Masahiro added. "We will sign them immediately."

"My uncles are very gracious and kind," Shigeru said. "I thank you."

"There is another matter, Shigeru, in which we seek your cooperation."

I had dropped to the floor again. My heart lurched in my throat. I wanted to warn him in some way, but of course I could not speak.

"You are aware of our negotiations with the Tohan. We feel alliance is preferable to war. We know your opinion. You are still young enough to be rash. . . ."

"At nearly thirty years, I can no longer be called young." Again Shigeru stated this fact calmly, as though there could be no arguing with it. "And I have no desire for war for its own sake. It is not the alliance that I object to as such: It is the current nature and conduct of the Tohan."

His uncles made no response to this remark, but the atmosphere in the room chilled a little. Shigeru also said nothing more. He had made his viewpoint clear enough—

too clear for his uncles' liking. Lord Masahiro made a sign to the steward, who clapped his hands quietly, and a few moments later tea appeared, brought by a maid who might have been invisible. The three Otori lords drank. I was not offered any.

"Well, the alliance is to go forward," Lord Shoichi said eventually. "Lord Iida has proposed that it be sealed by a marriage between the clans. His closest ally, Lord Noguchi, has a ward. Lady Shirakawa Kaede is her name."

Shigeru was admiring the teacup, holding it out in one hand. He placed it carefully on the matting in front of him and sat without moving a muscle.

"It is our desire that Lady Shirakawa become your wife," Lord Masahiro said.

"Forgive me, Uncle, but I have no desire to marry again. I have had no thoughts of marriage."

"Luckily you have relatives who will think of it for you. This marriage is greatly desired by Lord Iida. In fact, the alliance depends on it."

Lord Shigeru bowed. There was another long silence. I could hear footsteps coming from far away, the slow, deliberate tread of two people, one carrying something. The door behind us slid open and a man stepped past me and dropped to his knees. Behind him came a servant carrying a lacquer writing table, with ink block and brush and red vermilion paste for the seals.

"Ah, the adoption papers!" Lord Shoichi said genially. "Bring them to us."

The secretary advanced on his knees and the table was set before the lords. The secretary then read the agreement aloud. The language was flowery but the content was simple enough: I was entitled to bear the name of Otori and to receive all the privileges of a son of the household. In the event of children being born to a subsequent marriage, my rights would be equal to theirs, but not greater. In return I agreed to act as a son to Lord Shigeru, to accept his authority, and to swear allegiance to the Otori clan. If he died with no other legal heir, I would inherit his property.

The lords took up the seals.

"The marriage will be held in the ninth month," Masahiro said, "when the Festival of the Dead is over. Lord Iida wishes it to take place in Inuyama itself. The Noguchi are sending Lady Shirakawa to Tsuwano. You will meet her there and escort her to the capital."

The seals seemed to my eyes to hang in the air, suspended by a supernatural power. There was still time for me to speak out, to refuse to be adopted on such terms, to warn Lord Shigeru of the trap that had been set for him. But I said nothing. Events had moved beyond human control. Now we were in the hands of destiny.

"Shall we affix the seal, Shigeru?" Masahiro said with infinite politeness.

Lord Shigeru did not hesitate for a moment. "Please do so," he said. "I accept the marriage, and I am happy to be able to please you."

So the seals were affixed, and I became a member of the Otori clan and Lord Shigeru's adopted son. But as the seals of the clan were pressed to the documents, we both knew that they sealed his own fate.

By the time we returned to the house, the news of my adoption had been borne on the wind ahead of us, and everything had been prepared for celebration. Lord Shigeru and I both had reasons to be less than wholehearted, but he seemed to put whatever misgivings he had about marriage aside and

to be genuinely delighted. So was the whole household. I realized that I had truly become one of them over the months I had
been with them. I was hugged, caressed, fussed over, and plied
with red rice and Chiyo's special good-luck tea, made from
salted plum and seaweed, until my face ached with smiling
and the tears I had not shed from grief filled my eyes for joy.

Lord Shigeru had become even more worthy of my love
and loyalty. His uncles' treachery towards him had outraged
me on his behalf, and I was terrified about the plot they had
now laid against him. Then there was the question of the
one-armed man. Throughout the evening I felt Kenji's eyes
on me: I knew he was waiting to hear what I had learned, and
I was longing to tell him and Lord Shigeru. But by the time
the beds were spread out and the servants had retired, it was
past midnight, and I was reluctant to break the joyful mood
with bad tidings. I would have gone to bed saying nothing,
but Kenji, the only one of us who was truly sober, stopped
me when I went to douse the lamp, saying, "First you must
tell us what you heard and saw."

"Let it wait till morning," I said.

I saw the darkness that had lain behind Shigeru's gaze
deepen. I felt an immense sadness come over me, sobering me

completely. He said, "I suppose we must learn the worst."

"What made the horse shy?" Kenji asked.

"My own nervousness. But as he shied I saw the one-armed man."

"Ando. I saw him too. I did not know if you had, you gave no sign of it."

"Did he recognize Takeo?" Lord Shigeru asked immediately.

"He looked carefully at both of you for an instant and then pretended to have no further interest. But just the fact that he is here suggests he had heard something." He looked at me and went on, "Your peddler must have talked!"

"I am glad the adoption is legal now," Shigeru said. "It gives you a certain amount of protection."

I knew I had to tell him of the conversation I had overheard, but I was finding it hard even to speak of their baseness. "Forgive me, Lord Otori," I began. "I heard your uncles speaking privately."

"While you were counting—or miscounting—the household, I suppose," he replied dryly. "They were discussing the marriage?"

"Who is to be married?" Kenji said.

"I seem to have been contracted into a marriage to seal the alliance with the Tohan," Shigeru replied. "The lady in question is a ward of Lord Noguchi; Shirakawa is her name."

Kenji raised his eyebrows but did not speak. Shigeru went on, "My uncles made it clear that Takeo's adoption depended on this marriage." He stared into the darkness and said quietly, "I am caught between two obligations. I cannot fulfill both, but I cannot break either."

"Takeo should tell us what the Otori lords said," Kenji murmured.

I found it easier to speak to him. "The marriage is a trap. It is to send Lord Shigeru away from Hagi, where his popularity and opposition to the Tohan alliance may split the clan. Someone called Arai is challenging Iida in the West. If the Otori were to join him, Iida would be caught between them." My voice tailed away, and I turned to Shigeru. "Lord Otori knows all this?"

"I am in contact with Arai," he said. "Go on."

"Lady Shirakawa has the reputation of bringing death to men. Your uncles plan to . . ."

"Murder me?" His voice was matter-of-fact.

"I should not have to report so shameful a thing," I muttered, my face burning. "It was they who paid Shintaro."

Outside, the cicadas shrilled. I could feel sweat forming on my forehead, it was so close and still, a dark night with no moon or stars. The smell of the river was rank and muddy, an ancient smell, as ancient as treachery.

"I knew I was no favorite with them," Shigeru said. "But to send Shintaro against me! They must think I am really dangerous." He clapped me on the shoulder. "I have a lot to thank Takeo for. I am glad he will be with me in Inuyama."

"You're joking," Kenji exclaimed. "You cannot take Takeo there!"

"It seems I must go, and I feel safer if he is with me. Anyway, he is my son now. He must accompany me."

"Just try and leave me behind!" I put in.

"So you intend to marry Shirakawa Kaede?" Kenji said.

"Do you know her, Kenji?"

"I know of her. Who doesn't? She's barely fifteen and quite beautiful, they say."

"In that case, I'm sorry I can't marry her." Shigeru's voice was light, almost joking. "But it will do no harm if everyone thinks I will, for a while at least. It will divert Iida's attention, and will give us a few more weeks."

"What prevents you from marrying again?" Kenji said. "You spoke just now of the two obligations you are caught between. Since you agreed to the marriage in order that the adoption should go ahead, I understand that Takeo stands first with you. You're not secretly married already, are you?"

"As good as," Shigeru admitted after a pause. "There is someone else involved."

"Will you tell me who?"

"I have kept it secret for so long, I'm not sure I can," Shigeru replied. "Takeo can tell you, if he knows."

Kenji turned to me. I swallowed and whispered, "Lady Maruyama?"

Shigeru smiled. "How long have you known?"

"Since the night we met the lady at the inn in Chigawa."

Kenji, for the first time since I'd known him, looked really startled. "The woman Iida burns for, and wants to marry? How long has it been going on for?"

"You won't believe me," Shigeru replied.

"A year? Two?"

"Since I was twenty."

"That must be nearly ten years!" Kenji seemed as impressed by the fact that he had known nothing about the affair as by the news itself. "Yet another reason for you to hate Iida." He shook his head in amazement.

"It is more than love," Shigeru said quietly. "We are allies as well. Between them, she and Arai control the Seishuu and the southwest. If the Otori join them, we can defeat Iida." He paused and then went on, "If the Tohan take over the Otori domain, we will see the same cruelty and persecution that I rescued Takeo from in Mino. I cannot stand by and watch Iida impose his will on my people, see my country devastated, my villages burned. My uncles—Iida himself—know that I would never submit to that. So they mean to remove me from the scene. Iida has invited me into his lair, where he almost certainly intends to have me killed. I intend to use this to my advantage. What better way, after all, to get into Inuyama?"

Kenji stared at him, frowning. I could see Shigeru's open-hearted smile in the lamplight. There was something irresistible about him. His courage made my own heart catch fire. I understood why people loved him.

"These are things that do not concern the Tribe," Kenji said finally.

"I've been frank with you; I trust that all this will go no

further. Lady Maruyama's daughter is a hostage with Iida. Apart from that, more than your secrecy, I would be grateful for your help."

"I would never betray you, Shigeru, but sometimes, as you yourself said, we find ourselves with divided loyalties. I cannot pretend to you that I am not of the Tribe. Takeo is Kikuta. Sooner or later the Kikuta will claim him. There is nothing I can do about that."

"It's up to Takeo to make that choice when the time comes," Shigeru said.

"I have sworn allegiance to the Otori clan," I said. "I will never leave you, and I will do anything you ask of me."

For I was already seeing myself in Inuyama, where Lord Iida Sadamu lurked behind his nightingale floor.

· 6 ·

Kaede left Noguchi castle with no regrets and few hopes for the future, but since she had hardly been beyond its walls in the eight years she had been a hostage with the Noguchi, and since she was only fifteen, she could not help but be entranced by everything she saw. For the first few miles she and Lady Maruyama were carried in palanquins by teams of porters, but the swaying motion made her feel sick, and at the first rest stop she insisted on getting out and walking with Shizuka. It was high summer; the sun was strong. Shizuka tied a shady hat on her head, and also held up a parasol over her.

"Lady Shirakawa must not appear before her husband as brown as I am." She giggled.

They traveled until midday, rested for a while at an inn, and then went on for another few miles before evening. By the time they stopped, Kaede's mind was reeling with all she had seen: the brilliant green of the rice fields, as smooth and luxuriant as the pelt of an animal; the white splashing rivers that raced beside the road; the mountains that rose before them, range after range, clad in their rich summer green, interwoven with the crimson of wild azaleas. And the people on the road, of every sort and description: warriors in armor, bearing swords and riding spirited horses; farmers carrying all manner of things that she'd never seen before; oxcarts and packhorses, beggars and peddlers.

She was not supposed to stare at them, and they were supposed to bow to the ground as the procession went past, but she sneaked as many looks at them as they did at her.

They were accompanied by Lady Maruyama's retainers; the chief among them, a man named Sugita, treated the lady with the easy familiarity of an uncle. Kaede found that she liked him.

"I liked to walk when I was your age," Lady Maruyama

said as they ate the evening meal together. "I still prefer it, to be truthful, but I also fear the sun."

She gazed at Kaede's unlined skin. She had been kind to her all day, but Kaede could not forget her first impression, that the older woman did not like her and that in some way she had offended her.

"You do not ride?" she asked. She had been envying the men on their horses: They seemed so powerful and free.

"Sometimes I ride," Lady Maruyama replied. "But when I am a poor defenseless woman traveling through Tohan land, I allow myself to be carried in the palanquin."

Kaede looked questioningly at her. "Yet, Lady Maruyama is said to be powerful," she murmured.

"I must hide my power among men," she replied, "or they will not hesitate to crush me."

"I have not been on a horse since I was a child," Kaede admitted.

"But all warriors' daughters should be taught to ride!" Lady Maruyama exclaimed. "Did the Noguchi not do so?"

"They taught me nothing," Kaede said with bitterness.

"No use of the sword and knife? No archery?"

"I did not know women learned such things."

"In the West they do." There was a short silence. Kaede, hungry for once, took a little more rice.

"Did the Noguchi treat you well?" the lady asked.

"In the beginning, no, not at all." Kaede felt herself torn between her usual guarded response to anyone who questioned her, and a strong desire to confide in this woman, who was of the same class as she was and who was her equal. They were alone in the room, apart from Shizuka and Lady Maruyama's woman, Sachie, who both sat so still Kaede was hardly aware of them. "After the incident with the guard, I was moved to the residence."

"Before that?"

"I lived with the servant girls in the castle."

"How shameful," Lady Maruyama said, her own voice bitter now. "How do the Noguchi dare? When you are Shirakawa . . ." She looked down and said, "I fear for my own daughter, who is held hostage by Lord Iida."

"It was not so bad when I was a child," Kaede said. "The servants pitied me. But when the springtime began, and I was neither child nor woman, no one protected me. Until a man had to die . . ."

To her own astonishment, her voice faltered. A sudden

rush of emotion made her eyes fill with tears. The memory came flooding back to her: the man's hands, the hard bulge of his sex against her, the knife in her hand, the blood, his death before her eyes.

"Forgive me," she whispered.

Lady Maruyama reached across the space between them and took her hand. "Poor child," she said, stroking Kaede's fingers. "All the poor children, all the poor daughters. If only I could free you all."

Kaede wanted nothing more than to sob her heart out. She struggled to regain control. "After that, they moved me to the residence. I was given my own maid, first Junko, then Shizuka. Life was much better there. I was to be married to an old man. He died, and I was glad. But then people began to say that to know me, to desire me, brings death."

She heard the other woman's sharp intake of breath. For a moment neither of them spoke.

"I do not want to cause any man's death," Kaede said in a low voice. "I fear marriage. I do not want Lord Otori to die because of me."

When Lady Maruyama replied, her voice was thin. "You must not say such things, or even think them."

Kaede looked at her. Her face, white in the lamplight, seemed filled with a sudden apprehension.

"I am very tired," the lady went on. "Forgive me if I do not talk more tonight. We have many days on the road together, after all." She called to Sachie. The food trays were removed and the beds spread out.

Shizuka accompanied Kaede to the privy and washed her hands when she had finished there.

"What did I say to offend her?" Kaede whispered. "I don't understand her: One moment she is friendly, the next she stares at me as if I were poison to her."

"You're imagining things," Shizuka said lightly. "Lady Maruyama is very fond of you. Apart from anything else, after her daughter, you are her closest female relative."

"Am I?" Kaede replied and, when Shizuka nodded emphatically, asked, "Is that so important?"

"If anything happened to them, it is you who would inherit Maruyama. No one's told you this, because the Tohan still hope to acquire the domain. It's one of the reasons why Iida insisted you should go to the Noguchi as a hostage."

When Kaede said nothing, Shizuka went on, "My lady is even more important than she thought she was!"

"Don't tease me! I feel lost in this world. I feel as if I know nothing!"

Kaede went to bed, her mind swirling. She was aware of Lady Maruyama's restlessness through the night as well, and the next morning the lady's beautiful face looked tired and drawn. But she spoke to Kaede kindly and, when they set out, arranged for a gentle brown horse to be provided for her. Sugita lifted her onto its back, and at first one of the men walked at its head, leading it. She remembered the ponies she had ridden as a child and the ability began to come back. Shizuka would not let her ride for the whole day, saying her muscles would ache too much and she would be too tired, but she loved the feeling of being on the horse's back, and could not wait to mount again. The rhythm of its gait calmed her a little and helped her to organize her thoughts. Mostly she was appalled at her lack of education and her ignorance of the world she was entering. She was a pawn on the board of the great game the warlords were playing, but she longed to be more than that, to understand the moves of the game and to play it herself.

Two things happened to disturb her further. One afternoon they had paused for a rest at an unusual time, at a crossroads, when they were joined by a small group of horsemen riding from the southwest, almost as if by some prearranged appointment. Shizuka ran to greet them in her usual way, eager to know where they were from and what gossip they might bring. Kaede, watching idly, saw her speak to one of the men. He leaned low from the saddle to tell her something; she nodded with deep seriousness and then gave the horse a slap on its flank. It jumped forward. There was a shout of laughter from the men, followed by Shizuka's high-pitched giggle, but in that moment Kaede felt she saw something new in the girl who had become her servant, an intensity that puzzled her.

For the rest of the day Shizuka was her usual self, exclaiming over the beauties of the countryside, picking bunches of wildflowers, exchanging greetings with everyone she met, but at the lodging place that night Kaede came into the room to find Shizuka talking earnestly to Lady Maruyama, not like a servant, but sitting knee to knee with her, as an equal.

Their talk immediately turned to the weather and the next day's arrangements, but Kaede felt a sense of betrayal. Shizuka had said to her, *People like me don't really meet people like her*.

But there was obviously some relationship between them that she had known nothing about. It made her suspicious and a little jealous. She had come to depend on Shizuka and did not want to share her with others.

The heat grew more intense and travel more uncomfortable. One day the earth shook several times, adding to Kaede's unease. She slept badly, troubled as much by suspicions as by fleas and other night insects. She longed for the journey to end, and yet, she dreaded arriving. Every day she decided she would question Shizuka, but every night something held her back. Lady Maruyama continued to treat her with kindness, but Kaede did not trust her, and she responded cautiously and with reserve. Then she felt ungracious and childish. Her appetite disappeared again.

Shizuka scolded her at night in the bath. "All your bones stick out, lady. You must eat! What will your husband think?"

"Don't start talking about my husband!" Kaede said hurriedly. "I don't care what he thinks. Maybe he will hate the sight of me and leave me alone!"

And then she was ashamed again for the childishness of the words.

They came at last to the mountain town of Tsuwano,

riding through the narrow pass at the end of the day, the ranges already black against the setting sun. The breeze moved through the terraced rice fields like a wave through water, lotus plants raised their huge jade-green leaves, and around the fields wildflowers blossomed in a riot of color. The last rays of the sun turned the white walls of the town to pink and gold.

"This looks like a happy place!" Kaede could not help exclaiming.

Lady Maruyama, riding just ahead of her, turned in the saddle. "We are no longer in Tohan country. This is the beginning of the Otori fief," she said. "Here we will wait for Lord Shigeru."

The next morning Shizuka brought strange clothes instead of Kaede's usual robes.

"You are to start learning the sword, lady," she announced, showing Kaede how to put them on. She looked at her with approval. "Apart from the hair, Lady Kaede could pass for a boy," she said, lifting the heavy weight of hair away from Kaede's face and tying it back with a leather cord.

Kaede ran her hands over her own body. The clothes were of rough, dark-dyed hemp, and fitted her loosely. They were like nothing she had ever worn. They hid her shape and made her feel free. "Who says I am to learn?"

"Lady Maruyama. We will be here several days, maybe a week, before the Otori arrive. She wants you to be occupied, and not fretting."

"She is very kind," Kaede replied. "Who will teach me?"

Shizuka giggled and did not answer. She took Kaede across the street from their lodgings to a long, low building with a wooden floor. Here they removed their sandals and put on split-toed boots. Shizuka handed Kaede a mask to protect her face, and took down two long wooden poles from a rack on the wall.

"Did the lady ever learn to fight with these?"

"As a child, of course," Kaede replied. "Almost as soon as I could walk."

"Then you will remember this." Shizuka handed one pole to Kaede and, holding the other firmly in both hands, executed a fluid series of movements, the pole flashing through the air faster than the eye could follow.

"Not like that!" Kaede admitted, astonished. She would have thought Shizuka hardly able to lift the pole, let alone wield it with such power and skill.

Shizuka giggled again, changing under Kaede's eyes from concentrated warrior to scatterbrained servant. "Lady Kaede will find it all comes back! Let's begin."

Kaede felt cold, despite the warmth of the summer morning. "You are the teacher?"

"Oh, I only know a little, lady. You probably know just as much. I don't suppose there's anything I can teach you."

But even though Kaede found that she did remember the movements, and had a certain natural ability and the advantage of height, Shizuka's skill far surpassed anything she could do. At the end of the morning she was exhausted, dripping with sweat and seething with emotion. Shizuka, who as a servant did everything in her power to please Kaede, was completely ruthless as a teacher. Every stroke had to be perfectly executed. Time after time, when Kaede thought she was finally finding the rhythm, Shizuka would stop her and politely point out that her balance was on the wrong foot, or that she had left herself open to sudden death, had they been fighting with the sword. Finally she signaled that they should finish, placed the poles back in the rack, took off the face masks, and wiped Kaede's face with a towel.

"It was good," she said. "Lady Kaede has great skill. We

will soon make up for the years that were lost."

The physical activity, the shock of discovering Shizuka's skill, the warmth of the morning, the unfamiliar clothes, all combined to break down Kaede's self-control. She seized the towel and buried her face in it as sobs racked her.

"Lady," Shizuka whispered, "lady, don't cry. You have nothing to fear."

"Who are you really?" Kaede cried. "Why are you pretending to be what you are not? You told me you did not know Lady Maruyama!"

"I wish I could tell you everything, but I cannot yet. But my role here is to protect you. Arai sent me for that purpose."

"You know Arai too? All you said before was that you were from his town."

"Yes, but we are closer than that. He has the deepest regard for you, feeling himself to be in your debt. When Lord Noguchi exiled him, his anger was extreme. He felt himself insulted by Noguchi's distrust as well as his treatment of you. When he heard you were to be sent to Inuyama to be married, he made arrangements for me to accompany you."

"Why? Will I be in danger there?"

"Inuyama is a dangerous place. Even more so now, when the Three Countries are on the brink of war. Once the Otori alliance is settled by your marriage, Iida will fight the Seishuu in the West."

In the bare room, sunlight slanted through the dust raised by their feet. From beyond the lattice windows Kaede could hear the flow of water in the canals, the cries of street sellers, the laughter of children. That world seemed so simple and open, with none of the dark secrets that lay beneath her own.

"I am just a pawn on the board," she said bitterly. "You will sacrifice me as swiftly as the Tohan would."

"No, Arai and I are your servants, lady. He has sworn to protect you, and I obey him." She smiled, her face suddenly vivid with passion.

They are lovers, Kaede thought, and felt again a pang of jealousy that she had to share Shizuka with anyone else. She wanted to ask, *What about Lady Maruyama? What is her part in this game? And the man I am to marry?* But she feared the answer.

"It's too hot to do more today," Shizuka said, taking the towel from Kaede and wiping her eyes. "Tomorrow I'll teach you how to use the knife."

As they stood she added, "Don't treat me any differently. I am just your servant, nothing more."

"I should apologize for the times I treated you badly," Kaede said awkwardly.

"You never did!" Shizuka laughed. "If anything, you were far too lenient. The Noguchi may have taught you nothing useful, but at least you did not learn cruelty from them."

"I learned embroidery," Kaede said, "but you can't kill anyone with a needle."

"You can," Shizuka said offhandedly. "I'll show you one day."

For a week they waited in the mountain town for the Otori to arrive. The weather grew heavier and more sultry. Storm clouds gathered every night around the mountain peaks, and in the distance lightning flickered, yet it did not rain. Every day Kaede learned to fight with the sword and the knife, starting at daybreak, before the worst of the heat, and training for three hours at a stretch, the sweat pouring off her face and body.

Finally, one day at the end of the morning, as they were rinsing their faces with cold water, above the usual sounds of the streets came the tramp of horses, the barking of dogs.

Shizuka beckoned Kaede to the window. "Look! They are here! The Otori are here."

Kaede peered through the lattice. The group of horsemen approached at a trot. Most of them wore helmets and armor, but on one side rode a bareheaded boy not much older than herself. She saw the curve of his cheekbone, the silky gleam of his hair.

"Is that Lord Shigeru?"

"No." Shizuka laughed. "Lord Shigeru rides in front. The young man is his ward, Lord Takeo."

She emphasized the word *lord* in an ironic way that Kaede would recall later, but at the time she hardly noticed, for the boy, as if he had heard his name spoken, turned his head and looked towards her.

His eyes suggested depths of emotion, his mouth was sensitive, and she saw in his features both energy and sadness. It kindled something in her, a sort of curiosity mixed with longing, a feeling she did not recognize.

The men rode on. When the boy disappeared from sight

she felt she had lost a part of herself. She followed Shizuka back to the inn like a sleepwalker. By the time they got there, she was trembling as if with fever. Shizuka, completely misunderstanding, tried to reassure her.

"Lord Otori is a kind man, lady. You mustn't be afraid. No one will harm you."

Kaede said nothing, not daring to open her mouth, for the only word she wanted to speak was his name. *Takeo*.

Shizuka tried to get her to eat—first soup to warm her, then cold noodles to cool her—but she could swallow nothing. Shizuka made her lie down. Kaede shivered beneath the quilt, her eyes bright, her skin dry, her body as unpredictable to her as a snake.

Thunder crackled in the mountains and the air swam with moisture.

Alarmed, Shizuka sent for Lady Maruyama. When she came into the room an old man followed her.

"Uncle!" Shizuka greeted him with a cry of delight.

"What happened?" Lady Maruyama said, kneeling beside Kaede and placing her hand on her forehead. "She is burning; she must have taken a chill."

"We were training," Shizuka explained. "We saw the

Otori arrive, and she seemed to be struck by a sudden fever."

"Can you give her something, Kenji?" Lady Maruyama asked.

"She dreads the marriage," Shizuka said quietly.

"I can cure a fever, but that I cannot cure," the old man said. "I'll have them brew some herbs. The tea will calm her."

Kaede lay perfectly still with her eyes closed. She could hear them clearly, but they seemed to speak from another world, one that she had been plucked out of the moment her eyes met Takeo's. She roused herself to drink the tea, Shizuka holding her head as if she were a child, and then she drifted into a shallow sleep. She was woken by thunder rolling through the valley. The storm had finally broken and rain was pelting down, ringing off the tiles and sluicing the cobbles. She had been dreaming vividly, but the moment she opened her eyes the dream vanished, leaving her only with the lucid knowledge that what she felt was love.

She was astonished, then elated, then dismayed. At first she thought she would die if she saw him, then that she would die if she didn't. She berated herself: How could she have fallen in love with the ward of the man she was to marry? And then she thought: *What marriage?* She could not marry Lord Otori. She would marry no one but Takeo. And then she found herself laughing at her own stupidity. As if anyone married for love. *I've been overtaken by disaster*, she thought at one moment, and at the next, *How can this feeling be a disaster?*

When Shizuka returned she insisted that she had recovered. Indeed, the fever had abated, replaced by an intensity that made her eyes glow and her skin gleam.

"You are more beautiful than ever!" Shizuka exclaimed as she bathed and dressed her, putting on the robes that had been prepared for her betrothal, for her first meeting with her future husband.

Lady Maruyama greeted her with concern, asking after her health, and was relieved to find she was recovered. But Kaede was aware of the older woman's nervousness as she followed her to the best room in the inn, which had been prepared for Lord Otori.

She could hear the men talking as the servants slid the doors open, but they fell silent at the sight of her. She bowed to the floor, conscious of their gaze, not daring to look at any of them. She could feel every pulse in her body as her heart began to race.

"This is Lady Shirakawa Kaede," Lady Maruyama said. Her voice was cold, Kaede thought, and again wondered what she had done to offend the lady so much.

"Lady Kaede, I present you to Lord Otori Shigeru," Lady Maruyama went on, her voice now so faint it could hardly be heard.

Kaede sat up. "Lord Otori," she murmured, and raised her eyes to the face of the man she was to marry.

"Lady Shirakawa," he replied with great politeness. "We heard you were unwell. You are recovered?"

"Thank you, I am quite well." She liked his face, seeing kindness in his gaze. *He deserves his reputation*, she thought. *But how can I marry him?* She felt color rise in her cheeks.

"Those herbs never fail," said the man sitting on his left. She recognized the voice of the old man who had had the tea made for her, the man Shizuka called Uncle. "Lady Shirakawa has the reputation of great beauty, but her reputation hardly does her justice."

Lady Maruyama said, "You flatter her, Kenji. If a girl is not beautiful at fifteen, she never will be."

Kaede felt herself flush even more.

"We have brought gifts for you," Lord Otori said. "They

pale beside your beauty, but please accept them as a token of my deepest regard and the devotion of the Otori clan. Takeo."

She thought he spoke the words with indifference, even coldness, and imagined he would always feel that way towards her.

The boy rose and brought forward a lacquered tray. On it were packages wrapped in pale pink silk crepe, bearing the crest of the Otori. Kneeling before Kaede, he presented it to her.

She bowed in thanks.

"This is Lord Otori's ward and adopted son," Lady Maruyama said. "Lord Otori Takeo."

She did not dare look at his face. She allowed herself instead to gaze on his hands. They were long-fingered, supple, and beautifully shaped. The skin was a color between honey and tea, the nails tinged faintly lilac. She sensed the stillness within him, as if he were listening, always listening.

"Lord Takeo," she whispered.

He was not yet a man like the men she feared and hated. He was her age; his hair and skin had the same texture of youth. The intense curiosity she had felt before returned. She longed to know everything about him. Why had Lord Otori adopted him? Who was he really? What had happened to make him so sad? And why did she think he could hear her heart's thoughts?

"Lady Shirakawa." His voice was low, with a touch of the East in it.

She had to look at him. She raised her eyes and met his gaze. He stared at her, almost puzzled, and she felt something leap between them, as though somehow they had touched across the space that separated them.

The rain had eased a little earlier, but now it began again, with a drumming roar that all but drowned their voices. The wind rose, too, making the lamp flames dance and the shadows loom on the walls.

May I stay here forever, Kaede thought.

Lady Maruyama said sharply. "He has met you, but you have not been introduced: This is Muto Kenji, an old friend of Lord Otori, and Lord Takeo's teacher. He will help Shizuka in your instruction."

"Sir," she acknowledged him, glancing at him from under her eyelashes. He was staring at her in outright admiration, shaking his head slightly as if in disbelief. *He seems like a nice old man*, Kaede thought, and then: *But he is not so old after all!* His face seemed to slip and change in front of her eyes.

She felt the floor beneath her move with the very slightest of tremors. No one spoke, but from outside someone shouted in surprise. Then there was only the wind and the rain again.

A chill came over her. She must let none of her feelings show. Nothing was as it seemed.

ACKNOWLEDGMENTS

The main characters, Takeo and Kaede, came into my head on my first trip to Japan in 1993. Many people have helped me research and realize their story. I would like to thank the Asialink Foundation, who awarded me a fellowship in 1999 to spend three months in Japan, the Australia Council, the Department of Trade and Foreign Affairs and the Australian Embassy in Tokyo, and ArtsSA, the South Australian Government Arts Department. In Japan I was sponsored by Yamaguchi Prefecture's Akiyoshidai International Arts Village whose staff gave me invaluable help in exploring the landscape and the history of Western Honshuu. I would particularly like to thank Mr. Kori Yoshinori, Ms. Matsunaga Yayoi, and Ms. Matsubara Manami. I am especially grateful to Mrs. Tokorigi Masako for showing me the Sesshu paintings and gardens and to her husband, Miki, for information on horses in the medieval period.

Spending time in Japan with two theater companies gave me many insights—deepest thanks to Kazenoko in Tokyo and Kyushuu and Gekidan Urinko in Nagoya, and to Ms. Kimura Miyo, a wonderful traveling companion, who accompanied me to Kanazawa and the Nakasendo and who has answered many questions for me about language and literature.

I thank Mr. Mogi Masaru and Mrs. Mogi Akiko for their help with research, their suggestions for names, and, above all, their ongoing friendship.

In Australia I would like to thank my two Japanese teachers, Mrs. Thuy Coombes and Mrs. Etsuko Wilson; Simon Higgins, who made some invaluable suggestions; my agent, Jenny Darling; my son Matt, my first reader on all three books; and the rest of my family for not only putting up with but sharing my obsessions.

I would also like to acknowledge the insights and expert knowledge of the samurai history archive on the World Wide Web and members of the discussion forum.

Calligraphy was drawn for me by Ms. Sugiyama Kazuko and Etsuko Wilson. I am immensely grateful to them.

TURN THE PAGE FOR A PREVIEW OF

ACROSS THE

Nightingale Floor

·1·

After my formal adoption into the clan, I began to see more of the young men of my own age from warrior families. Ichiro was much sought after as a teacher, and since he was already instructing me in history, religion, and the classics, he agreed to take on other pupils as well. Among these was Miyoshi Gemba, who, with his older brother, Kahei, was to become one of my closest allies and friends. Gemba was a year older than me. Kahei was already in his twenties, and too old for Ichiro's instruction, but he helped teach the younger men the arts of war.

For these I now joined the men of the clan in the great hall opposite the castle, where we fought with poles and studied other martial arts. On its sheltered southern side was a wide field for horsemanship and archery. I was no better with the bow than I'd ever been, but I could acquit myself well enough with the pole and the sword. Every morning, after two hours of writing practice with Ichiro, I would ride with a couple of men through the winding streets of the castle town and spend four or five hours in relentless training.

In the late afternoons I returned to Ichiro with his other pupils, and we struggled to keep our eyes open while he tried to teach us the principles of Kung Tzu and the history of the Eight Islands. The summer solstice passed, and the Festival of the Weaver Star, and the days of the great heat began. The plum rains had ended, but it remained very humid, and heavy storms threatened. The farmers gloomily predicted a worse than usual typhoon season.

My lessons with Kenji also continued, but at night. He stayed away from the clan hall, and warned me against revealing my Tribe skills.

"The warriors think it's sorcery," he said. "They'll despise you for it."

We went out on many nights, and I learned to move invisibly through the sleeping town. We had a strange relationship. I did not trust him at all in daylight. I'd been adopted by the Otori, and I'd given my heart to them. I did not want to be reminded that I was an outsider, even a freak. But it was different at night. Kenji's skills were unparalleled. He wanted to share them with me, and I was mad with hunger to learn them—partly for their own sake, because they fulfilled some dark need that was born into me, and partly because I knew how much I had to learn if I was ever to achieve what Lord Shigeru wanted me to do. Although he had not yet spoken of it to me, I could think of no other reason why he had rescued me from Mino. I was the son of an assassin, a member of the Tribe, now his adopted son. I was going with him to Inuyama. What other purpose could there be but to kill Iida?

Most of the boys accepted me, for Shigeru's sake, and I realized what a high regard they and their fathers had for him. But the sons of Masahiro and Shoichi gave me a hard time, especially Masahiro's oldest son, Yoshitomi. I grew to hate them as much as I hated their fathers, and I despised them, too, for their arrogance and blindness. We often fought with the poles. I knew their intentions towards me were murderous. Once Yoshitomi would have killed me if I had not in an instant used my second self to distract him. He never forgave me for it and often whispered insults to me: Sorcerer. Cheat. I was actually less afraid of him killing me than of having to kill him in self-defense or by accident. No doubt it improved my swordsmanship, but I was relieved when the time for our departure came and no blood had been shed.

It was not a good time for traveling, being in the hottest days of summer, but we had to be in Inuyama before the Festival of the Dead began. We did not take the direct highway through Yamagata, but went south to Tsuwano, now the outpost town of the Otori fief, on the road to the West, where we would meet the bridal party and where the betrothal would take place. From there we would cross into Tohan territory and pick up the post road at Yamagata.

Our journey to Tsuwano was uneventful and enjoyable despite the heat. I was away from Ichiro's teaching and from the pressures of training. It was like a holiday, riding in Shigeru and Kenji's company, and for a few days we all seemed to put aside our misgivings of what lay ahead. The rain held off, though lightning flickered round the ranges all night, turning the clouds indigo, and the full summer foliage of the forests surrounded us in a sea of green.

We rode into Tsuwano at midday, having risen at sunrise for the last leg of the journey. I was sorry to arrive, knowing it meant the end of the innocent pleasures of our lighthearted travel. I could not have imagined what was going to take their place. Tsuwano sang of water, its streets lined with canals teeming with fat golden and red carp. We were not far from the inn when suddenly, above the water and the sounds of the bustling town, I clearly heard my own name spoken by a woman. The voice came from a long, low building with white walls and lattice windows, some kind of fighting hall. I knew there were two women inside but I could not see them, and I wondered briefly why they were there, and why one of them should have said my name.

When we came to the inn I heard the same woman talking in the courtyard. I realized she was Lady Shirakawa's maid, and we learned the lady was unwell. Kenji went to her and came back wanting to describe her beauty at length, but the storm broke, and I was afraid the thunder would make the horses restive, so I hurried off to the stables without listening to him. I did not want to hear of her beauty. If I thought about her at all, it was with dislike, for the part she was to play in the trap set for Shigeru.

After a while Kenji caught up with me in the stables, and brought the maid with him. She looked like a pretty, good-natured, scatterbrained girl, but even before she grinned at me in a less than respectful way and addressed me as "Cousin!" I'd picked her as a member of the Tribe.

She held her hands up against mine. "I am also Kikuta, on my mother's side. But Muto on my father's. Kenji is my uncle."

Our hands had the same long-fingered shape and the same line straight across the palm. "That's the only trait I inherited," she said ruefully. "The rest of me is pure Muto."

Like Kenji, she had the power to change her appearance so that you were never sure you recognized her. At first I thought she was very young; in fact she was almost thirty and had two sons.

"Lady Kaede is a little better," she told Kenji. "Your tea made her sleep, and now she insists on getting up."

"You worked her too hard," Kenji said, grinning. "What were you thinking of, in this heat?" To me he added, "Shizuka is teaching Lady Shirakawa the sword. She can teach you too. We'll be here for days in this rain."

He turned back to her. "Maybe you can teach him ruthlessness," he said. "It's all he lacks."

"It's hard to teach," Shizuka replied. "You either have it, or not."

"She has it," Kenji told me. "Stay on her right side!"

I didn't reply. I was a little irritated that Kenji should point out my weakness to Shizuka as soon as we met her. We stood under the eaves of the stable yard, the rain drumming on the cobbles before us, the horses stamping behind.

"Are these fevers a common thing?" Kenji asked.

"Not really. This is the first of its kind. But she is not strong. She hardly eats; she sleeps badly. She frets over the marriage and over her family. Her mother is dying, and she has not seen her since she was seven."

"You have become fond of her," Kenji said, smiling.

"Yes, I have, although I only came to her because Arai asked me to."

"I've never seen a more beautiful girl," Kenji admitted.

"Uncle! You are really smitten by her!"

"I must be getting old," he said. "I find myself moved by her plight. However things work out, she will be the loser."

A huge clap of thunder broke over our heads. The horses bucked and plunged on their lines. I ran to quiet them. Shizuka returned to the inn and Kenji went in search of the bathhouse. I did not see them again until evening.

Later, bathed and dressed in formal robes, I attended on
Lord Shigeru for the first meeting with his future wife. We
had brought gifts, and I unpacked them from the boxes,
together with the lacquerware that we carried with us. A
betrothal should be a happy occasion, I suppose, although I
had never been to one before. Maybe for the bride it is always
a time of apprehension. This one seemed to me to be fraught
with tension and full of bad omens.

Lady Maruyama greeted us as if we were no more than
slight acquaintances, but her eyes hardly left Shigeru's face. I
thought she had aged since I'd met her in Chigawa. She was
no less beautiful, but suffering had etched her face with its
fine lines. Both she and Shigeru seemed cold, to each other
and to everyone else, especially to Lady Shirakawa.

Her beauty silenced us. Despite Kenji's enthusiasm
earlier, I was quite unprepared for it. I thought then that I
understood Lady Maruyama's suffering: At least part of it
had to be jealousy. How could any man refuse the possession
of such beauty? No one could blame Shigeru if he accepted
it: He would be fulfilling his duty to his uncles and the
demands of the alliance. But the marriage would deprive

Lady Maruyama of not only the man she had loved for years but also her strongest ally.

The undercurrents in the room made me uncomfortable and awkward. I saw the pain Lady Maruyama's coldness caused Kaede, saw the flush rise in her cheeks, making her skin lovelier than ever. I could hear her heartbeat and her rapid breath. She did not look at any of us, but kept her eyes cast down. I thought, *She is so young, and terrified*. Then she raised her eyes and looked at me for a moment. I felt she was like a person drowning in the river, and if I reached out my hand I would save her.

"So, Shigeru, you have to choose between the most powerful woman in the Three Countries and the most beautiful," Kenji said later while we were sitting up talking, and after many flasks of wine had been shared. Since the rain seemed likely to keep us in Tsuwano for some days, there was no need to go to bed early in order to rise before dawn. "I should have been born a lord."

"You have a wife, if only you stayed with her," Shigeru replied.

"My wife is a good cook, but she has a wicked tongue, she's fat, and she hates traveling," Kenji grumbled. I said nothing, but laughed to myself, already knowing how Kenji profited from his wife's absence: in the pleasure quarter.

Kenji continued to joke, with, I thought, some deeper purpose of sounding Shigeru out, but the lord replied to him in the same vein, as if he truly were celebrating his betrothal. I went to sleep, fuddled by the wine, to the sound of rain pelting on the roof, cascading down the gutters and over the cobbles. The canals ran to the brim; in the distance I could hear the song of the river grow to a shout as it tumbled down the mountain.

I woke in the middle of the night and was immediately aware that Shigeru was no longer in the room. When I listened I could hear his voice, talking to Lady Maruyama, so low that no one could hear it but me. I had heard them speak like that nearly a year before, in another inn room. I was both appalled at the risk they were taking and amazed at the strength of the love that sustained them through such infrequent meetings.

He will never marry Shirakawa Kaede, I thought, but did not know if this realization delighted me or alarmed me.

I was filled with unease and lay awake till dawn. It was a gray, wet dawn, too, with no sign of any break in the weather. A typhoon, earlier than usual, had swept across the western part of the country, bringing downpours, floods, broken bridges, impassable roads. Everything was damp and smelled of mold. Two of the horses had hot, swollen hocks, and a groom had been kicked in the chest. I ordered poultices for the horses and arranged for an apothecary to see the man. I was eating a late breakfast when Kenji came to remind me about sword practice. It was the last thing I felt like doing.

"What else do you plan to do all day," he demanded, "sit around and drink tea? Shizuka can teach you a lot. We might as well make the most of being stuck here."

So I obediently finished eating and followed my teacher, running through the rain to the fighting school. I could hear the thump and clash of the sticks from outside. Inside, two young men were fighting. After a moment I realized one was not a boy but Shizuka: She was more skillful than her opponent, but the other, taller and with greater determination, was making it quite a good match. At our appearance, though, Shizuka easily got beneath the guard. It wasn't until the other took off the mask that I realized it was Kaede.

11

"Oh," she said angrily, wiping her face on her sleeve, "they distracted me."

"Nothing must distract you, lady," Shizuka said. "It's your main weakness. You lack concentration. There must be nothing but you, your foe, and the swords."

She turned to greet us. "Good morning, Uncle! Good morning, Cousin!"

We returned the greeting and bowed more respectfully to Kaede. Then there was a short silence. I was feeling awkward: I had never seen women in a fighting hall before—never seen them dressed in practice clothes. Their presence unnerved me. I thought there was probably something unseemly about it. I should not be here with Shigeru's betrothed wife.

"We should come back another time," I said, "when you have finished."

"No, I want you to fight with Shizuka," Kenji said. "Lady Shirakawa can hardly return to the inn alone. It will profit her to watch."

"It would be good for the lady to practice against a man," Shizuka said, "since if it comes to battle, she will not be able to choose her opponents."

I glanced at Kaede and saw her eyes widen slightly, but she said nothing.

"Well, she should be able to beat Takeo," Kenji said sourly. I thought he must have a headache from the wine, and indeed, I myself felt a little the worse for wear.

Kaede sat on the floor, cross-legged like a man. She untied the ties that held back her hair and it fell around her, reaching the ground. I tried not to look at her.

Shizuka gave me a pole and took up her first stance.

We sparred a bit, neither of us giving anything away. I'd never fought with a woman before, and I was reluctant to go all out in case I hurt her. Then, to my surprise, when I feinted one way she was already there, and a twisting upwards blow sent the pole out of my hands. If I'd been fighting Masahiro's son, I'd have been dead.

"Cousin," she said reprovingly. "Don't insult me, please."

I tried harder after that, but she was skillful and amazingly strong. It was only after the second bout that I began to get the upper hand, and then only after her instruction. She conceded the fourth bout, saying, "I have already fought all morning with Lady Kaede. You are fresh, Cousin, as well as being half my age."

"A little more than half, I think!" I panted. Sweat was pouring off me. I took a towel from Kenji and wiped myself down.

Kaede said, "Why do you call Lord Takeo 'Cousin'?"

"Believe it or not, we are related, on my mother's side," Shizuka said. "Lord Takeo was not born an Otori, but adopted."

Kaede looked seriously at the three of us. "There is a likeness between you. It's hard to place exactly. But there is something mysterious, as though none of you is what you seem to be."

"The world being what it is, that is wisdom, lady," Kenji said, rather piously, I thought. I imagined he did not want Kaede to know the true nature of our relationship: that we were all from the Tribe. I did not want her to know either. I much preferred her to think of me as one of the Otori.

Shizuka took up the cords and tied back Kaede's hair. "Now you should try against Takeo."

"No," I said immediately. "I should go now. I have to see to the horses. I must see if Lord Otori needs me."

Kaede stood. I was aware of her trembling slightly, and acutely aware of her scent, a flowery fragrance with her sweat beneath it.

"Just one bout," Kenji said. "It can't do any harm."

Shizuka went to put on Kaede's mask, but she waved her away.

"If I am to fight men, I must fight without a mask," she said.

I took up the pole reluctantly. The rain was pouring down even more heavily. The room was dim, the light greenish. We seemed to be in a world within a world, isolated from the real one, bewitched.

It started like an ordinary practice bout, both of us trying to unsettle the other, but I was afraid of hitting her face, and her eyes never left mine. We were both tentative, embarking on something utterly strange to us whose rules we did not know. Then, at some point I was hardly aware of, the fight turned into a kind of dance. Step, strike, parry, step. Kaede's breath came more strongly, echoed by mine, until we were breathing in unison, and her eyes became brighter and her face more glowing, each blow became stronger, and the rhythm of our steps fiercer. For a while I would dominate, then she, but neither of us could get the upper hand. Did either of us want to?

Finally, almost by mistake, I got around her guard and,

to avoid hitting her face, let the pole fall to the ground. Immediately, Kaede lowered her own pole and said, "I concede."

"You did well," Shizuka said, "but I think Takeo could have tried a little harder."

I stood and stared at Kaede, open-mouthed like an idiot. I thought, *If I don't hold her in my arms now, I will die.*

Kenji handed me a towel and gave me a rough push in the chest. "Takeo . . ." he started to say.

"What?" I said stupidly.

"Just don't complicate things!"

Shizuka said, as sharply as if she were warning of danger, "Lady Kaede!"

"What?" Kaede said, her eyes still fixed on my face.

"I think we've done enough for one day," Shizuka said. "Let's return to your room."

Kaede smiled at me, suddenly unguarded. "Lord Takeo," she said.

"Lady Shirakawa." I bowed to her, trying to be formal, but utterly unable to keep myself from smiling back at her.

"Well, that's torn it," Kenji muttered.

"What do you expect, it's their age!" Shizuka replied. "They'll get over it."

As Shizuka led Kaede from the hall, calling to the servants who were waiting outside to bring umbrellas, it dawned on me what they were talking about. They were right in one thing, and wrong in another. Kaede and I had been scorched by desire for each other, more than desire, love, but we would never get over it.

For a week the torrents of rain kept us penned up in the mountain town. Kaede and I did not train together again. I wished we had never done so: It had been a moment of madness, I had never wanted it, and now I was tormented by the results. I listened for her all day long, I could hear her voice, her step, and at night—when only a thin wall separated us—her breathing. I could tell how she slept (restlessly) and when she woke (often). We spent time together—we were forced to by the smallness of the inn, by being in the same traveling party, by being expected to be with Lord Shigeru and Lady Maruyama—but we had no opportunity to speak to each other. We were both, I think, equally terrified of giving our feelings away. We hardly dared look at each other, but occasionally our eyes would meet, and the fire leaped between us again.

I went lean and hollow-eyed with desire, made worse by lack of sleep, for I reverted to my old Hagi ways and went exploring at night. Shigeru did not know, for I left while he was with Lady Maruyama, and Kenji either did not or pretended not to notice. I felt I was becoming as insubstantial as a ghost. By day I studied and drew; by night I went in search of other people's lives, moving through the small town like a shadow. Often the thought came to me that I would never have a life of my own, but would always belong to the Otori or to the Tribe.

I watched merchants calculating the loss the water damage would bring them. I watched the townspeople drink and gamble in bars and let prostitutes lead them away by the arm. I watched parents sleep, their children between them. I climbed walls and drainpipes, walked over roofs and along fences. Once I swam the moat, climbed the castle walls and gate, and watched the guards, so close I could smell them. It amazed me that they did not see or hear me. I listened to people talking, awake and in their sleep, heard their protestations, their curses, and their prayers.

I went back to the inn before dawn, drenched to the skin, took off my wet clothes, and slipped naked and shivering beneath the quilts. I dozed and listened to the place waking around me. First the cocks crowed, then the crows began cawing; servants woke and fetched water; clogs clattered over the wooden bridges; Raku and the other horses whinnied from the stables. I waited for the moment when I would hear Kaede's voice.

The rain poured down for three days and then began to lessen. Many people came to the inn to speak to Shigeru. I listened to the careful conversations and tried to discern who was loyal to him and who would be only too eager to join in his betrayal. We went to the castle to present gifts to Lord Kitano, and I saw in daylight the walls and gate I had climbed at night.

He greeted us with courtesy and expressed his sympathy for Takeshi's death. It seemed to be on his conscience, for he returned to the subject more than once. He was of an age with the Otori lords and had sons the same age as Shigeru. They did not attend the meeting. One was said to be away, the other unwell. Apologies were expressed, which I knew were lies.

"They lived in Hagi when they were boys," Shigeru told me later. "We trained and studied together. They came many times to my parents' house and were as close as brothers to Takeshi and myself." He was silent for a moment, then went on: "Well, that was many years ago. Times change and we must all change with them."

But I could not be so resigned. I felt bitterly that the closer we came to Tohan territory, the more isolated he was becoming.

It was early evening. We had bathed and were waiting for the meal. Kenji had gone to the public bathhouse, where a girl had taken his fancy, he said. The room gave on to a small garden. The rain had lessened to a drizzle and the doors were wide open. There was a strong smell of sodden earth and wet leaves.

"It will clear tomorrow," Shigeru said. "We will be able to ride on, but we will not get to Inuyama before the festival. We will be forced to stay in Yamagata, I think." He smiled entirely mirthlessly and said, "I shall be able to commemorate my brother's death in the place where he died. But I cannot let anyone know my feelings. I must pretend to have put aside all thought of revenge."